"Do you smell a conspiracy?"

"As if someone is trying to force us together?" Rachel asked.

"Yeah." One eye squinted, Jake scratched the side of his short beard. "Maybe."

"As in *matchmaking*?" Her expression widened, incredulous, maybe a tad horrified. "Between us?"

He hitched a shoulder and waited, thinking exactly that.

Rachel's dark hair swished back and forth on her shoulders as she disagreed. "That's impossible. Our friends and family know we divorced. You've remarried, had a child."

Except they were both single now.

"No argument here. But still, I'm suspicious."

Rachel's mouth flattened. "How do we stop them?"

"I don't know." Jake bent back the flaps on a cardboard box marked Props. "Maybe the fact that we keep running into each other really *is* coincidental."

"When did you start believing in coincidence?"

"Never." That she recalled this minutia pleased him. "God's the director of my path, not chance."

"So you're saying God is bringing us together?"

Would that be so terrible?

Jake sighed. Apparently, she thought so.

Linda Goodnight, a *New York Times* bestselling author and winner of a RITA® Award in Inspirational Fiction, has appeared on the Christian bestseller list. Her novels have been translated into more than a dozen languages. Active in orphan ministry, Linda enjoys writing fiction that carries a message of hope in a sometimes-dark world. She and her husband live in Oklahoma. Visit her website, lindagoodnight.com, for more information.

Books by Linda Goodnight

Love Inspired

A Mommy for Easter

Sundown Valley

To Protect His Children
Keeping Them Safe
The Cowboy's Journey Home
Her Secret Son
To Protect His Brother's Baby

The Buchanons

Cowboy Under the Mistletoe
The Christmas Family
Lone Star Dad
Lone Star Bachelor

Love Inspired Trade

Claiming Her Legacy

Visit the Author Profile page at LoveInspired.com for more titles.

A Mommy
for Easter

Linda Goodnight

LOVE INSPIRED
INSPIRATIONAL ROMANCE

LOVE INSPIRED®
INSPIRATIONAL ROMANCE

Recycling programs for this product may not exist in your area.

ISBN-13: 978-1-335-59722-9

A Mommy for Easter

Copyright © 2024 by Linda Goodnight

For questions and comments about the quality of this book, please contact us at CustomerService@Harlequin.com.

Love Inspired
22 Adelaide St. West, 41st Floor
Toronto, Ontario M5H 4E3, Canada
www.LoveInspired.com

Printed in U.S.A.

But I would not have you to be ignorant, brethren,
concerning them which are asleep, that ye
sorrow not, even as others which have no hope.
For if we believe that Jesus died and rose again,
even so them also which sleep in Jesus
will God bring with him.

—1 Thessalonians 4:13–14

This book is lovingly dedicated to the silent sufferers of pregnancy loss and to my grandbabies in Heaven. You are not forgotten.

Chapter One

She'd been warned.

Doors should be locked, especially at night, even in a friendly, quiet little town like Rosemary Ridge.

But Rachel Hamby sometimes forgot. In this safe, peaceful neighborhood, she always assumed the doors and windows were locked until discovering they weren't. Last night, apparently, one of them wasn't.

Therefore, she should not have been surprised on that early spring morning when she stumbled into the kitchen to find someone already there.

Asleep.

On the gray tile floor.

With a well-loved stuffed rabbit snuggled under her tiny chin, her purple-footed pajamas dotted with pink puppies.

A very little girl.

Rachel knew most of her neighbors and this child did not belong to any of them.

Where had she come from? What was she doing here?

Suddenly, Rachel no longer needed coffee. A jolt of adrenaline charged through her veins, enough to keep her running for days. Weeks, maybe.

The girl was a toddler, perhaps two or three. Delicate

brown curls bunched at the base of her neck, her long lashes curved over smooth round cheeks. She sucked one ear of the toy gray rabbit.

Rachel's chest squeezed with regret and loss.

At thirty-eight, she'd given up hope of ever having children, of ever finding Mr. Right. And definitely of ever having a child of her own fall asleep on the kitchen floor.

Quietly, she pulled a chair from the island and perched on the edge to watch the sleeping toddler.

"Where did you come from, baby girl?"

Her baby, had he lived, would have passed through this stage and looked just as adorable. Rachel was certain of it because hadn't he been beautiful even at fifteen weeks' gestation, when the nurse had handed his tiny body to her on a blue towel?

That was the first and last time she ever saw her baby. She still wondered what happened to those who died before full term. No one had given her an option. They simply whisked him away. Out of sight, out of mind, which was not true at all.

Not a day went by that she didn't think about that tiny son and also about his father, about the awful mistakes they'd made in their inability to cope with the loss of a child they'd both wanted. Eventually, they'd fallen apart. She still blamed him, and she'd kept a painful secret that no one but her ever needed to know. Would he have cared? She didn't think so.

Last she'd heard, he had remarried after leaving Rosemary Ridge to finish his education.

Learning that he had moved on with his life while she was stuck in her loss had been an excruciating blow. He hadn't cared enough about their son to grieve for long. Or about her.

She wondered if he now had those children they'd once planned to have together.

Rachel gave her shoulders a shake. All of that was water under the bridge. Revisiting old hurts didn't help this little lost toddler one bit. She was long past the self-pity stage, the recriminations, the questions. Life flowed onward. She was a busy woman with plenty of friends and extended family, including a mother and brother who depended on her to handle anything they didn't want to. After all, she didn't have a husband or children to look after. Her brother, Paul, did.

Most of the time she didn't mind their requests. Or those of the church and town. She enjoyed being needed. Like now, for instance. Today she had a busy schedule, including a meeting with the Rosemary Ridge Easter Committee to decide when, where and how the town would welcome spring and honor Resurrection Sunday.

So much to do. But the small intruder on her kitchen tile came first.

The child stirred.

Long lashes fluttered up, then down and then up again.

Tugging the rabbit closer, she whimpered something unintelligible.

Rachel's heart clutched like a fist in her chest. Poor precious. She must be frightened to wake in a strange place.

Leaving her chair, Rachel knelt beside the child and brushed the soft curls away from her forehead.

The action must have startled the child for she sat upright and blinked around the room in confusion.

Rachel's hand fell away.

"Hello, sweetheart. Can you tell me your name?"

Wide eyes, the color of honey, grew glassy. "I want Daddy."

"Who are your mama and daddy, honey? Where are they? I'll help you find them."

Going silent, the child pulled her bunny rabbit closer and stuck the tip of its ear in her mouth.

"Are you hungry? Thirsty?"

The brown curls bobbed in acquiescence.

Okay, that was a good start. What did she have that a toddler would eat?

Going to the refrigerator, Rachel looked inside. She didn't cook much these days, but the peach yogurt looked promising. She took it out and carried the carton to the island.

"Do you like yogurt?"

The child didn't answer but rose to her feet and toddled over in her footed, blanket pajamas.

March grew warmer with each passing day, but the nights could be cool or downright cold. Whoever this child belonged to had dressed her properly for the weather. She looked clean and well nourished. Loved.

Someone must surely be looking for this baby.

"And probably scared out of their wits."

Rachel fished in her robe pocket for her cell phone, found the number and called.

"Rosemary Ridge Police Department. What is your emergency?"

"Alice, this is Rachel Hamby." In a town this size, it wasn't surprising that she and the day dispatcher knew each other.

"Hi, Rachel, is anything wrong?"

"Not really but kind of. Is Chief Ambruster in?"

"Sure. Hold on."

She heard Alice's megaphone voice yell, "Chief, it's Rachel Hamby."

After several beeps, the chief came on. Rachel advised him of the situation.

"Asleep on your kitchen floor, you say? That's a call I don't take too often. Is she hurt?"

"She looks fine to me, still in her pajamas, with a stuffed animal in hand."

"Huh. Okay. That's good. She must have wandered away from a nearby home somehow. Kids do that. The other officers are out on calls, but I'll be over shortly. Keep her there until I arrive."

Keep her here? What else would she do with a toddler? Set her out in the street with a cardboard lost-and-found sign?

All she said was, "Thanks, Chief."

As she hung up, a small someone tugged on her robe. "I need go potty."

Oh. Of course, she did. Which made Rachel wonder how long she'd had been asleep on the kitchen tile.

Taking the small hand, she led the toddler to the bathroom. The little girl stood inside, door open, staring back at Rachel.

Didn't she know what to do from here?

When the child kept waiting, Rachel asked, "Do you need help?"

One bob of the head was her answer.

No problem. She taught a children's Sunday school class and volunteered in Wednesday night nursery. She understood little kids.

Except none of them came dressed in footie pajamas.

"Here you go, precious. I'll help."

She took care of the girl's needs and then lifted her up to wash her hands.

The child felt as light as a poodle puppy. Soft and sweet scented like baby lotion, she triggered a range of emotions in Rachel.

Before she realized what she was doing, Rachel pressed her face against the soft spot at the back of the tiny neck and breathed her in. She wondered if she'd ever stop long-ing to enjoy that sweet scent on a child of her own.

Some things weren't meant to be. Hadn't her mother told her that a hundred times? She'd wrestled that adage until she was worn thin, but the fact remained, she'd never remarried or had the family she wanted. Mom—and that tired old saying—must be right.

Before she could tumble into an abyss of self-pity and allow her mind to replay the awful days of pregnancy loss, she carried the girl back to the kitchen. The island was too high for a toddler. She might fall, so Rachel moved her to the living room coffee table with peach yogurt and a cup of water.

Sitting on the couch with the child on the floor on her knees, Rachel kept up a running chatter about the stuffed bunny, upcoming Easter and anything else she could think of to keep the child happy until help arrived. Bunny rabbit lay on the carpet beside the little girl.

By the time the yogurt was gone, a car door slammed outside the town house.

"A nice policeman is here, honey. He'll help you find your mama." Rachel led the child to the door and opened it to reveal Chief Ambruster coming up the sidewalk.

Unlike the stereotypical police chief, the head of Rose-mary Ridge's police department might be on the far north side of fifty but he was lean and fit. A close friend and sometimes golf partner of her dad, Rachel knew him well. Clint Ambruster exemplified the Protect and Serve motto emblazoned on his SUV.

Police gear rattled and a shoulder radio squawked as he approached the door.

"Cute little thing, isn't she? Do you recognize her?" he asked.

"No. I was hoping you would."

"I don't, so I'll have to put in a call to child services over in the county seat. A social worker will come get her while we put out the lost-child alert."

"That could take hours. What do we do with her in the meantime?"

"I'll take her down to the station. Alice will ply her with doughnuts and let her play games on her phone. Chances are, someone will wake up this morning, realize she's gone and call the police before the social worker gets here."

Although Rachel knew Chief was right, she still said, "I wouldn't mind keeping her with me, but what you say is true. No one would come looking for her here at my house."

Chief, who was a grandfather to several, went to one bended knee. "What's your name, sugar pea?"

"Dawey." The word was whispered in such a small voice, Rachel strained to understand.

Chief looked to Rachel for interpretation.

"I think she said Terri."

"Okay, Terri—" the chief held out a big hand "—come with Chief Pawpaw and we'll find your mama and daddy."

As trusting as could be, Terri placed her teensy hand in the policeman's big one.

Rachel walked along on the other side, one hand resting gently against the child's back.

Chief asked, "You going to the Easter meeting this afternoon?"

"Yes. We're setting up subcommittees today but still looking for better ideas. You got any?"

"Me?" He chuckled. "Nope. Sarah's the smart one in my family. I leave all that business up to her. I just show up with traffic control and security."

Rachel patted his arm. "We couldn't do this without you, Chief, or without Sarah." The chief's wife was chair of all things Easter and as such, wrangled business people and town volunteers like Rachel into working long, unpaid hours "for the good of the town and the glory of God."

"Seventy-fifth anniversary of a big event is somethin' to celebrate, all right." He turned loose of Terri's hand and reached for the back door of the vehicle. "All right, little Miss Terri, let's give you a ride in Chief Pawpaw's big car."

Just as he was opening the SUV door, a man's voice came from somewhere to their left.

"Daley! Daley!"

Chief paused, one hand on the child's shoulder and the other on the handle.

Rachel spun toward the sound.

All she saw was a big furry dog charging toward her at full speed. She braced for impact.

Before Rachel could decide if the dog was friend or foe, Terri squealed, the lab skidded to a stop in front of her, and the child threw both arms around the animal's neck.

"Moose. Moose."

"I think she knows this dog," Rachel said.

"Seems like the dog sure knows her," Chief said in his easygoing drawl. "And I figure that fella yellin' his lungs out down the street just might know her too."

Jake Colter thought he might lose his mind or maybe go into cardiac arrest as he raced frantically down the street in the still-sleeping neighborhood, screaming Daley's name.

He'd lost her.

How on earth had he lost his daughter in the middle of the night in a town as strange to her as Timbuktu?

A chill ran through him as the worst-case scenario intruded.

The back patio door had been standing wide open.

Had someone abducted her?

Too many terrifying cases of exactly such a thing made the news these days. The world was a frightening place, especially for a man raising a little girl in a new town.

He'd been gone too long to be comfortable in the reassurance that nothing bad ever happened in Rosemary Ridge. That was back then. This was now.

The world had changed, and definitely not for the better, in the many years since he'd moved away. No doubt Rosemary Ridge had changed with it.

Since becoming a dad, nothing scared him more than the thought of a child predator.

Pausing briefly, hands on his knees, to suck air into his oxygen-deprived lungs, Jake murmured, "Not my baby, Lord. Please, keep her safe. She's all I have."

He prayed a half dozen jumbled prayers, all of them pleas for mercy and help and safety. Daley was so small, so innocent.

Oblivious to the chilly spring morning, the charming tree-blossomed neighborhood and the colorful tulips and daffodils waving from flower beds and around trees, he kicked into a sprint again, his heart pounding with every rapid footfall.

"Where is she, Jesus? Help me. Show me. Bring her back safely."

Other parents of lost children must have prayed these same desperate prayers. He didn't like thinking that some of them went unanswered.

He knew how painful unanswered prayers could be.

Huffing, puffing, sick to his stomach with fear, his hastily donned athletic shoes came untied. This time, he didn't pause. He let them flop. One short rest was all he needed. Adrenaline stoked by fear fueled him.

He, who easily and with confident assurance, calmed

the panicked owners of sick or injured dogs and cats, was about to come apart at the seams.

As he rounded a car parked in a driveway that blocked his sight line, he spotted what appeared to be a police vehicle, complete with gigantic, waving antenna on either side of the back end.

Police. Why hadn't he thought to call them?

Panic-fried brain, muddled thinking.

Now that he saw a police car, he aimed toward it. When the policeman stepped back from the vehicle, Jake spotted Moose, his dark red retriever.

Hanging on to the dog with a death grip was a child. In purple footies.

A bedraggled stuffed rabbit was slung across Moose's back.

Thank You, Jesus!

"Daley. Daley!"

Suddenly, a child's wail rose in the air. His child's. He'd know that cry anywhere.

Panting like one of his overheated canine patients, Jake fell to his knees beside the dog and child. In one quick, breathless grab, he clutched Daley against his pounding heart.

Eyes closed, he said a silent prayer of thanksgiving and praise. God had heard his plea.

This time, He had answered in Jake's favor.

Chapter Two

It couldn't be him. Not after all this time. This could not be Jake Colter. This guy had to be a doppelgänger, someone who resembled her ex-husband.

Rachel stood frozen to the sprouting green grass. An icy chill, which had nothing to do with the cool spring weather, flooded her body. She wrapped both arms around her waist and wished she'd remained inside the house, not out here in plain sight in her white wrap bathrobe.

Vulnerable, that's how she felt. Vulnerable and shocked to the toes of her fuzzy slip-on mules.

"This your little girl, mister?" Chief asked, casual-like but with enough frown to know he meant business. A lost or missing child was a serious situation.

"Yes, sir. This is my daughter, Daley." The man, who could not be Jake, rose with the toddler in his arms.

A gaggle of emotions struggled inside Rachel's chest. Her hands began to shake.

It was him. It was Jake. Why? How? What was he doing back in Rosemary Ridge, standing in her front yard? Especially after so many years of living elsewhere.

Time had been kind to him. For a man pushing forty, he'd kept his flat belly, likely still jogging and hitting the gym several times a week. He appeared to have also lost weight. When they'd been together, he'd jokingly complained that her cooking was too good to resist and he'd put on a few pounds. Those were gone now.

The smile lines around his brown eyes had deepened and faint worry lines creased his brow, although neither detracted from his good looks. He wore navy blue sweatpants and a mismatched emerald green hoody; his dark brown hair was longer than she remembered and apparently uncombed in this morning's haste. He'd grown facial hair, one of those scruffy, beard-mustache looks, like a Hallmark movie hero. Or maybe he simply hadn't had time to shave.

She didn't know if she liked the look or not, which didn't matter. *He* didn't matter. His daughter did.

Why oh why was he here in her town, her neighborhood?

While she tried to find her breath and restart her heart, Chief, unaware of her dilemma, said, "I'll need to see some ID, sir, before you take this child anywhere."

Jake blinked, flummoxed. "It's back at the house. When I realized Daley was gone from her bed and nowhere inside, I threw on my clothes and ran. The last thing on my mind was ID."

"Understandable," Chief said kindly, "but *you'll* understand why I need you and your daughter to ride back to your house with me and get that ID before I let you keep her."

"Absolutely. Glad to." Jake hugged the child closer. Daley, not *Terri* as she'd thought, snuggled into his neck and relaxed, the flop-eared rabbit dangling in one small hand. The big red dog sat at their feet, tongue lolling and his eyes never leaving his tiny charge.

"Whatever you need," Jake continued. "I'm thankful Daley was found safe and sound."

"You can thank Rachel for that." Chief jerked a thumb in her direction. "She discovered your little one asleep on her kitchen floor."

"Rachel?" For the first time, Jake moved his attention from the child and the chief to her. His mouth dropped open. He closed it. Something shifted in his eyes. Memories, caution. "Rachel? Is that you?"

Rachel finally came out of her stupor to squawk, "Jake?"

"You found Daley inside your house?"

Nodding, Rachel turned to Chief Ambruster and said, "Chief, you may not remember him, but this is Jake Colter. He grew up here." *And married me and lost a baby before running away.*

Bitterness she didn't know still existed rose up and left a nasty taste in her mouth.

If her heart pounded any harder, she'd faint. She needed to get away from him and find her bearings. This was too much too fast.

Jake wriggled a hand free from around his daughter and offered it to the chief. "We moved in yesterday. I'm the new vet. I'll be working with Doc Howell."

He'd moved back to Rosemary Ridge? He was the new vet? Why hadn't she heard about this? Her mother, who usually knew everything in the small town, had not said a word.

She *had* heard that Doc Howell, who was nearing retirement age and had a sickly wife, was looking for a partner in his veterinarian practice, but she didn't know he'd found one. And of all people, Jake Colter!

"You vouching for him, Rachel?" Chief asked.

She exchanged looks with Jake. Should she?

The terror in his voice and the worry in his handsome face got to her even if she didn't want it to. She'd loved this man once. Trusted him. He'd broken that trust and abandoned her when she'd needed him most.

"I'm sure it's no trouble for him to show you his ID. Just to be on the safe side. I didn't know he had a daughter." She wasn't being spiteful, was she? Only careful. The little girl deserved that. After all, Rachel didn't know Jake Colter anymore. If she ever had.

"Won't be any trouble for me to tote the two of you home," Chief said. "Where do you live, Doc?"

Jake pointed toward the back of her townhouse and beyond. "Straight through there. I'm the buff brick house directly across the alleyway."

Dismay settled like lead in Rachel's stomach.

What were the chances that her ex-husband and his family would move into one of the townhouse rentals behind her? "That explains how your daughter got to my place. She must have crossed the alley."

"She walks in her sleep sometimes, but this is the farthest she's ever gone. I guess the new situation confused her."

"Don't you lock your doors?"

"Don't you?" he shot back.

Rachel stiffened. Seeing him again was difficult enough without getting into an argument. She touched Daley's tiny back. "Bye, Daley. I like your rabbit." To the police officer, she said, "Thanks, Chief. I guess you don't need me anymore."

Chief patted her shoulder. "You go on. I know how busy you are. I got this."

She turned and started back toward her home.

"Rachel." Jake's voice stopped her.

She paused, looked back over her shoulder with a question in her expression. He stood there in the morning sun looking weary and frazzled and altogether too handsome.

She really didn't deserve this. God must be working on

her gift of long-suffering, even though she was pretty sure she'd suffered long enough.

"What?" she finally said, none too friendly.

What might have been the beginnings of a conciliatory smile teased the corners of her ex-husband's mouth for a second before sliding away. "Good to see you."

She couldn't say the same. So she didn't.

But the trip across her yard and back inside the house seemed twice as long as before.

She couldn't help wondering if Jake had followed her with his eyes.

Rachel.

Jake had known they'd run into each other again, now that he'd joined Doc Howell's animal practice and returned to Rosemary Ridge. After so many years, he had not expected the meeting to happen this way, with him running down the street, screaming like a madman for his lost daughter, and her in her cozy bathrobe.

Even rumpled from sleep, Rachel was still pretty. She'd let her dark hair grow to her shoulders, a new look that he liked. Which didn't matter. They were ancient history.

The thought of *them*, which he hadn't had in a long time, lay heavy in his chest.

As he and Daley, along with a delighted Moose, rode with the police chief, and even after he'd shown his ID along with Daley's birth certificate—a wonder he'd found the document in all the unpacked clutter of his new residence—his thoughts kept returning to Rachel, his first love. His first wife.

He'd been confident that he would not be affected by seeing her again. He thought he'd left all the heartaches of Rosemary Ridge behind. Otherwise, he would not have accepted Doc Howell's job offer.

He'd been wrong. Even with all the water that had flowed under the very wide bridge that now existed between Rachel and him, the waves of memory sloshing through him came with unexpected force.

Being pragmatic, he supposed no one ever fully recovered from a divorce, even if they'd married again and tried to be a better spouse this time.

He had his daughter, his vet practice and his faith in a God Who had carried him through the hardest times of his life. They were enough.

A man who'd failed twice at marriage was not fool enough to consider trying again. He was sadly sure that if Mallory had lived, she would have left him at some point. Sooner rather than later. Falling in love had been easy. Sadly, falling out of love had been even easier. He'd learned that the hard way—twice.

He was great at caring for animals. Women, not so much.

"Daddy."

"Yes, baby. You hungry?"

"I got yogurt."

"You want yogurt for breakfast? What about cereal?" Surely, he could locate a box of cereal within this jumble of moving boxes cluttering his small kitchen. Yogurt was out of the running for now. Grocery shopping was on today's to-do list. Along with unpacking and adding child safety locks to all his doors.

"No, Daddy. The wady gave me yogurt." Daley pronounced lady with a *W*, as she did most things containing the letter *L*.

Oh. Rachel had fed his little girl yogurt and looked after her until the police arrived. The action was like her, or the way she had been when he'd known her. She'd always had a soft spot for kids. Everyone's.

Had she remarried? Did she have that half dozen kids she'd wanted but they'd been unable to have?

With a sigh, he turned his attention to his daughter and tried to keep Rachel out of his head.

"Want to watch cartoons while I unpack?"

"I wike to help."

"Are you sure you're not hungry or thirsty?"

Her brown eyes brightened. "Can I have juice, please?"

He tapped her nose, still adrenaline-jacked from her morning escapade. She'd been unable to tell him how she'd gotten across the alley and into Rachel's house. Sleepwalking, for sure.

"One juice pouch coming up. Then we'll find you some clothes in all this and get dressed for the day. We need to unpack, go to the grocery store, stop at the bank and do some work around here before Monday. Want to visit my new animal hospital later?"

"Does they got puppies?" She was already nodding her head.

"Maybe. I'm not sure. We'll find out together."

One slender shoulder rose and fell in a shrug. "Okay."

Jake counted himself blessed that Daley was such an easy child. Except for her bad dreams and propensity for sleepwalking, she rarely caused a problem. Her pediatrician said she'd outgrow both, so he tried not to worry.

After handing off the drink, Jake began emptying moving boxes, starting with the personal items for Daley's room. Yesterday, he'd set up her bed, but her clothes remained in boxes. Somewhere.

After moving a few cartons, his gaze fell on one marked with Daley's name. He started up the stairs with it.

"Daddy?" Daley tagged alongside, dragging her bunny with one hand while holding the juice pouch with the other. Moose, the affable retriever who adored Daley, flashed past and waited happily at the top as if to say "Hurry up, slow-pokes."

"What?"

"I wike her. She's nice."

"Who?"

"The furry wady."

Jake bit back a laugh. Furry? "The lady who found you this morning?"

"She's nice. Can she come to us house and pway?"

Not a good idea, considering the evil eye Rachel had given him once she'd gotten over the shock of seeing him again. He held no animosity, but apparently, she still did. "She's probably busy, baby."

How did a man explain an ex-wife to a three-year-old?

Daley pulled a green pair of pants from the box and stuck them on her head. The legs flopped over like bunny ears.

She was a miniature comedian, this daughter of his, and enjoyed making him laugh with her antics. He did, hoping she was distracted from the topic of Rachel.

She wasn't.

"Can you ask her?"

"No." Before his daughter could hit him with a dozen more questions he couldn't answer, and the inevitable *why*, he got a reprieve. His cell phone chimed.

A quick glance at caller ID revealed his new boss's name.

"Good morning, Doc," he said.

"Good morning, Doc," came the reply.

They both chuckled softly at the old joke.

"Are you settled in yet?" Doc Howell asked.

"Not even close."

"Figured. You could hire someone to unpack and set things up for you."

"I'd never be able to find anything if I did that." Jake glanced at his daughter, now sitting inside her new closet trying on shoes from a box he'd stuck in there. Moose lay next to her, one paw on her thigh, close, as if worrying she'd disappear again on his watch. That's one of the things that surprised him about Daley's midnight jaunt. Somehow, Moose, usually Daley's shadow, had not been alerted.

"You still coming by the clinic this morning?" his new boss asked.

Jake glanced at the clock. "As planned. Got work for me to do already?"

"Yes, but not at the clinic."

"A farm call?" This was spring when livestock animals gave birth. Sheep and goats were notorious for needing help.

"Actually, an Easter call."

Jake poked a handful of toddler socks into the top drawer. "I don't think I'm following you."

Doc laughed. "Don't you remember how Rosemary Ridge goes all-out at Easter? 'Easter on steroids,' as Helen likes to say."

"No one can forget a Rosemary Ridge Easter celebration." This small town was serious about its celebrations, especially Easter and Christmas, thanks to a large co-op of churches.

"This year is the seventy-fifth anniversary of the event. The town is pulling out all the stops."

"I still don't know what this has to do with me and work."

"Normally, I sit on the Easter committee along with a slew of other business owners and townspeople, but with Helen's health issues—"

Jake got the drift. Helen was Doc's wife of many years and one of the reasons he wanted to semi-retire. "You want me to take your place."

"Exactly. They need new blood anyway. All of us are get-

ting long in the tooth and short on new ideas. Having someone take my spot would sure take a load off me. Can you be
there today at two?"

Today? Jake thought of the pile of unpacked boxes, the
grocery list and all the other things he had to do. But this
was a new job and he didn't want to start off on the wrong
foot. "How can I say no to my new boss?"

Doc Howell laughed. "Consider yourself on the clock,
starting at two. Deal?"

"I'm not sure what I can add, but I'll be there. Is it okay
if I take Daley?"

"Oh, sure, sure. No problem at all."

They finished the conversation with a few more details
and hung up.

Jake rubbed a hand over his scruffy whiskers.

Cancel most of his to-do list for the day. Looked like
he would be thinking about Easter egg hunts and Easter
pageants this afternoon.

Chapter Three

The meeting room in the fellowship hall of South Cross Church buzzed with conversation. Even though the meeting was for the town at large, the church offered its huge family center for a variety of meetings and events. Anything from scouting groups and family reunions to town meetings. Like this one.

The scent of coffee and doughnuts, the latter fresh-baked at the local Rise and Shine Doughnut Shop, made the cavernous space smell cozy and warm.

Someone—Rachel suspected it was Chief Ambruster's stocky, red-haired wife, Sarah—had already set up a projector screen and laptop computer for a quick review of last year's events. Long rectangular tables were organized so that everyone could see and hear everyone else.

Sarah Ambruster was a master organizer, though sometimes a little on the pushy side. She had a way of getting folks to do their part. Inevitably, she would threaten to have them arrested by her police-chief husband if they didn't cooperate, a joke that always brought a laugh along with that cooperation, however reluctant.

A microphone squealed as Mrs. Ambruster stepped to the center of the tables. "One more minute, folks. Grab your coffee and let's get started. Easter's right around the corner."

With her coffee and a maple glazed doughnut she didn't need, Rachel settled in next to her mother, Sue Ann Hamby, another consummate volunteer.

Claire Haskins, Rachel's best friend, slid into the chair on her opposite side. "I made it. Whew. What a day it's been."

"You don't know the half of it, Claire," Rachel said.

Her friend slanted her a frown. "What happened? You look upset."

"I ran into my ex-husband this morning. In my robe and slippers. Apparently, he now lives in the house directly behind mine."

Eyes widening, Claire gasped. "Jake's back?"

Rachel clutched her disposable coffee cup with both hands, hands that were still chilled from this morning's shock. "You didn't know, either?"

"No." She pointed toward Rachel's doughnut. "Are you going to eat that?" When Rachel shook her head, she took the pastry and bemoaned, "I never know anything except my boys' soccer schedules unless you tell me, but this is big news."

Her mother sipped her coffee and then slowly set aside the cup. "I might have heard something about that."

Rachel, in the middle of a sip, choked on her drink. She sputtered, got her breath and asked, "Mom! Seriously? Why didn't you tell me?"

"Why would I? The divorce was ages ago. Most people move on, Rachel, remarry, have a family. Many are even cordial with their exes."

Was Mom's comment a subtle way of saying Rachel was stuck in a rut?

Rachel bristled. "I *have* moved on. I just didn't appreciate the surprise of finding him in my front yard this morning. You let me get blindsided."

"What? Why was Jake Colter in your front yard?" Claire said a little too loudly.

Mom blinked. "Jake came to your house? Whatever for?"

"Long story."

Mom shot a glance at the chairwoman shuffling a stack of paper. "Tell it fast."

Claire took a giant bite of Rachel's doughnut and leaned in.

Rachel gave a quick synopsis of finding Daley on her kitchen floor, a police call and a frantic Jake running down the street in a mismatched sweat suit.

"How does he look?" Claire asked.

Rachel gave her a sharp glance. Claire responded with a wave of the half-eaten doughnut. "Never mind. Never mind. I hope he's wrinkled and ugly and covered in frog warts."

Both Rachel and Sue Ann laughed.

"Jake didn't stick around long enough for me to notice." Not true exactly. "He scooped up his daughter, and then Chief took them and their big red dog home."

"I didn't realize he had a child. Oh, Rach." Claire put a conciliatory hand on top of Rachel's. "Are you okay?"

Not really, but she put on a positive front, the way she'd been doing for years.

"As Mom said, it's normal for divorced people to remarry and have families." Which validated what Rachel had known since the divorce. She wasn't exactly normal.

Sarah Ambruster's microphone squeaked a warning. Rachel and her tablemates turned their attention to her.

That's when Rachel saw him. Directly across the U-opening at the opposing table.

Opposing being a very good word choice.

Jake Colter was at the meeting too.

"The nice wady is here, Daddy."

So he'd noticed.

Jake wasn't one to believe in fate or coincidence, but he'd been in Rosemary Ridge barely twenty-four hours and had encountered his ex-wife twice already. What were the chances?

The fact that she'd spotted him and then deliberately turned her head was telling. She didn't want to be friends or neighbors or have anything at all to do with him.

Okay. He got that. They hadn't exactly parted with goodbye hugs and a promise to write. Divorces, even mutual ones, meant failure and heartache. Still, they were going to be living in the same town and in the same general neighborhood. He hoped they could be civil.

Daley shook his arm. "Daddy, that wady wants you."

His heart jumped. "What? What lady?" Rachel?

Daley pointed an index finger toward the front.

After a few reality-check blinks, Jake realized the chairwoman had said his name. He made eye contact with her, hoping the question on his face was enough to encourage her to repeat whatever she'd said.

"Dr. Jake Colter, welcome back to Rosemary Ridge. We're thrilled to have you and your little girl with us. Dr. Howell let me know you'd be taking his place on the committee this year."

With his face hot with embarrassment, Jake nodded. He'd better stop thinking about Rachel and pay attention.

"Glad to help." Which might not be completely true, but he didn't want to get off on the wrong foot with his boss or the town. "Thank you for the welcome."

"What's your little girl's name?"

"Daley."

Mrs. Ambruster smiled. But then, looking at Daley's open, innocent expression could make anyone smile. "Everyone be sure to make Dr. Colter and Daley feel welcome when we break for subcommittees."

He knew one person who wouldn't, and that bothered him. He regretted the hurt they'd caused each other, but after all this time, Rachel's cold reception surprised him a little. Maybe it shouldn't have, but it did.

Wishing he'd grabbed a cup of coffee to give his hands something to do, Jake rotated his stiff shoulders and made sure Daley settled in with her crayons and coloring book. And stickers. His mouth curved with tenderness as he watched his dark-haired princess decorate a red-colored puppy dog with sparkly ice cream cone stickers.

Confident Daley was well occupied, he turned his attention to a video and a report about last Easter's successes and a discussion of areas they could improve and expand. Afterward, Sarah Ambruster, in her no-nonsense tone, announced the newly appointed subcommittees.

The main organizing group apparently had been hard at work since the new year, but now was the time to take those ideas and put them in action.

Jake half listened. He was new, so he expected to be assigned as a general helper to one of Doc Howell's former tasks. They would probably ask him to vet-check the animals entered in the parade or coordinate with the animal shelter for free pet adoptions. Those, he could handle, no problem.

"Because she did such an outstanding job last year, the egg hunt subcommittee will be chaired by Rachel Hamby. I'm sure she's discovered ways to make the event bigger, better, and more fun this year. She always does."

Jake's gaze slid to Rachel.

Hamby. He'd known she had retaken her maiden name, but Hamby instead of Colter, her name for seven years, still sounded strange to him.

Her head turned in profile, she didn't notice him staring, so he looked his fill, telling himself that he felt nothing for her anymore except regret and sadness that he had not been enough to heal her broken heart. The failure was in him, he knew now, although he'd not known back then.

She looked much the same as he remembered. Dressed in a faded denim jacket over a dark blue print dress. Simple, but pretty on her. He'd never been much for noticing a woman's clothes but he noticed Rachel's today.

"Members of Rachel's Eggstravaganza," Mrs. Ambruster continued, "include Claire Adams, the Myrick brothers and Dr. Colter."

She continued reading names Jake didn't recognize, but he knew without a glance in her direction that Rachel would not be pleased to find him as a member of her committee. Her iciness at both encounters was a pretty good indication that she wanted nothing to do with him.

"Rachel's group," the chairwoman said, "will be in charge of estimating the number of attendees—using last year's numbers, of course, which I have right here." She waved a printed page. "They'll also collect and stuff eggs, determine the age divisions, and procure prizes and supplies, hopefully from generous local businesses. The egg hunt is a major event, but I'm confident Rachel and her crew can handle every task without a problem."

Sarah aimed a smile and a wink at Rachel and handed her the to-do list. During the announcement, Rachel's pleased smile had melted away. Was her negative reaction because of him?

"As always, our coffers are limited, so twist a few arms for donations. Rachel will assign tasks and add other volunteers as she sees fit." Sarah showed her teeth in a you-will-do-this smile before continuing with other committee assignments.

Jake frowned toward the makeshift podium in the center of the tables. This was not what he'd expected nor what he thought he'd agreed to. He was a vet, not an arm-twisting donation collector or a plastic-egg stuffer.

He snuck another glance at Rachel. Her gray eyes met his. She was frowning too.

Jake drew in a long breath and sighed.

He was not getting off to a good start with his new neighbor.

"I guess she's forgotten," Rachel muttered quietly to her half-empty coffee cup. "Why else would Sarah put me in this uncomfortable position?"

Her mother heard her. "You endured Maggie Stiles on the church pageant committee last year, and she's impossible. You can certainly put up with the new vet. If you don't *make* an issue of Jake's inclusion, it won't *be* an issue."

The mention of Maggie Stiles elevated Rachel's mood—a little. "Maggie wanted to sing 'You're a Mean One, Mr. Grinch' in the church cantata."

"And have Pontius Pilate dressed like the Grinch."

"Complete with pointy, striped shoes, a Santa hat and a green face."

They grinned into each other's eyes. "You're right. I know you are."

"Good girl." Mom patted her arm. "You can do this. With grace and kindness, the way you do everything."

She could. But that didn't mean she'd be happy about it.

From Jake's frown he wasn't pleased either. Maybe she could convince Sarah to reassign Jake to another group.

And the moon would fall from the sky as sliced cheddar cheese.

Sarah did not like anyone to question her decisions unless one wanted to be seen as a poor sport who didn't love Easter. Or Jesus. Sarah had the ability to make Rachel feel as if she was turning her back on God Himself if she didn't want to do something. The woman was a master at guilt trips.

Poor Chief Ambruster. No wonder he didn't retire.

But Sarah's leadership and relentless work ethic never failed to produce a magnificent citywide event that incorporated churches, civic groups and her very own Easter committee. Advertising for the occasion had gone out a week ago, complete with an agenda for the entire Holy Week from Palm Sunday to Easter.

Who was she to squawk about her small part?

Mom was right. She could do this. Seeing Jake again so unexpectedly had rattled her. That's all. Once she realigned her attitude, she would be fine.

Grace and kindness.

With a little well-placed convincing, Jake would probably bow out anyway. A workaholic, he'd be too busy building his veterinary practice to help much, and she and the other volunteers would get the job done.

Still, why couldn't Jake be assigned to the parade or the advertising groups? Or lower Siberia?

When the group broke into subcommittees, Rachel ignored the dark-haired animal doctor who'd pulled a chair to the end of her table. He was to her right. She didn't have to look at him, but she knew he was there and knowing bothered her.

She should be over this. Everyone said so. But one glance at Jake, one mention of his name, and the agony of their lost future rolled in like a black cloud. The divorce didn't hurt so much anymore, but the other did.

Loss was a deep, dark chasm. Most of the time she was fine, but occasionally the what-ifs haunted her. Seeing Jake again stirred them to life.

Get over it, everyone said. *Move on. It was only a miscarriage.*

Only a miscarriage of every dream she'd ever dreamed.

Chairs scooted as coffee cups were refilled and members of the various committees gathered in groups. Rachel's team settled around her, eager to begin.

"All right, everyone," she said, still avoiding the right side of the table. "Looks like we have a good group, so we should be able to come up with fresh ideas. As always, we'll have the town's egg hunt in the city park on the Saturday afternoon before Easter. The parade will be that morning, but we'll let the parade committee handle all that and focus on our part. If you look at the agenda, you'll see many of the churches have pageants, musical events or special services throughout the week. One is having a sunrise service at daybreak on Easter, and of course the other churches will cap the week with more beautiful pageants or music and a special message."

"Wow," Claire said. "Our little town is doing a lot."

"Seventy-fifth anniversary," she reminded her best friend.

"Normally at the Eggstravaganza, we have some games along with music from one of the churches before and after the egg hunts. This year, Sarah has ordered in a few food trucks and a bounce house. I've already contacted four of the churches to prepare and man the games, and I have two more on my list to contact about creating a kids' craft area. Does that sound good to everyone?"

Claire's hand shot up. "Rachel, what if we added some contests?"

The afternoon was already crowded with activity, but a good leader never refused to listen. "I like the idea. What do you have in mind?"

"Like maybe an egg-decorating contest. If we get the word out to the schools, clubs and churches early, everyone can start working on their ideas and then bring their entries to the park tent for display and judging on that Saturday morning. I can get the shop to donate some prizes."

The owner of Kim's Flower and Gifts generously supplied prizes and gift certificates every year. Claire worked there, the reason her fingers were stained with chlorophyll green, although her ankle pants and off-the-shoulder sweater looked chic and trendy. A dancer in her youth, Claire still had a dancer's body.

"I love your idea, Claire." Rachel jotted contests on her notepad. "What do the rest of you think? All in favor?"

A murmur of agreement circled the table as hands rose. Rachel scanned the committee.

"Looks like we have an egg-citing new event." She grinned at her own joke, feeling more positive by the minute. Jake had remained mercifully quiet. She hadn't even had to look in his direction.

But she knew he was there.

That tiny tingle she got when someone was staring tickled the hairs on the back of her neck. Was it Jake?

Rachel chastised herself. What difference did it make if he stared? They were nothing to each other. Absolutely nothing. He'd remarried, had a beautiful little girl. Left her behind.

Stop it, Rachel. Stop it.

"And," Claire said, on a roll now that her idea had been enthusiastically received, "since this year's parade theme is An Old-fashioned Easter, why not give prizes for the fanciest or most well-decorated Easter bonnet?"

"That's a great idea, too," Rachel's mom said, nodding her perfectly coifed blond head. Sue Ann Hamby never missed her weekly appointment at the Hair Port. "Back in the day, ladies bought new outfits and really dressed up on Easter. A carefully chosen Easter bonnet was their crowning glory. It will be fun to bring that old tradition back to the holiday. We could add a section for men too. Old-fashioned fedoras, derbies, top hats and what-have-you would be such fun."

"I like that idea, Mom. What about the rest of you?"

Again, a murmur of agreement and upraised hands.

Rachel was getting excited now. This was easy. She had a great group. She loved doing this and could almost forget that her ex-husband was in the room. "We could ask parade marchers to wear an Easter bonnet or hat and judge the best in several categories as the floats are being judged."

A tiny voice interrupted the proceedings. "I gots a hat. Daddy buyed it. It's red."

Rachel's attention, momentarily diverted by the new ideas and not keen on looking at Jake, shot to Daley. The child, crayon in hand, looked up from her coloring book.

Jake leaned in to shush her. He looked tired.

A frisson of sympathy moved through Rachel. He was a good dad to let his daughter tag along, which made her wonder about Daley's mother.

So much for ignoring him.

With an apologetic lift of eyebrows, he said, "Sorry for the interruption."

Their gazes connected and Rachel's throat tightened with a strange, uncomfortable feeling.

This was beyond awkward. Did anyone else at the table feel the tension?

Not tension exactly but something disturbing.

She lowered her head and focused on the notepad lying on the table.

Her mom cleared her throat and removed her reading glasses, always a sign she was about to speak.

"This is a committee meeting, and if Daley has an idea, we want to hear it." To the little girl, she said, "Daley, honey, do you want to enter the hat contest too?"

Daley nodded her dark curls with enough enthusiasm to cause a chuckle among the group.

"There you have it then," her mom said. "We'll open the Easter bonnet contest to anyone who wishes to enter. All age groups." To Rachel she said, "Put me down as volunteering to figure out the details and round up judges."

"Great. Thanks, Mom." Rachel made a notation on her pad, careful not to look at Jake again.

The tired lines around his eyes and mouth bothered her. Worry lines too.

"Don't thank me," Mom said. "Thank Jake's adorable little girl. It's her idea."

Without looking up, Rachel said, "Thank you, Daley."

Throughout the meeting, Jake said nothing as first one, and then another, took on specific duties to organize the Saturday Eggstravaganza. Although another committee handled the parade, Rachel was confident they'd go for the Easter bonnet contest. She made a note to talk to the chairperson.

As her committee discussed various age groups for the egg hunts, Sheila Ramirez, a veteran high school teacher spoke up. "Is there anything we can do to include the teenagers more? We provide lots of kid events, which are great, but my high school students feel left out."

"Do they *want* to hunt eggs?" someone asked with enough doubt to indicate her opinion.

"Teenagers aren't interested in little kid games," said another.

Rumbles of agreement and remarks about teens being too cool or too old for fun bothered Rachel. "Wait, everyone. Surely, we can figure out a way to include interested teens. Easter is for everyone. Remember John 3:16?"

The table went silent.

Then a masculine voice tentatively said, "Here's a thought."

All eyes turned toward Jake, which meant Rachel was forced to look at him too.

Oh, my.

Little Daley perched her elbow on the table, her chin on her hand and stared at her dad with adoration.

The tender expression touched Rachel with bittersweet poignancy. Would their children have adored him too? She had, once upon a time. Until she'd learned who he really was.

"Teenagers like competition," he said. One hand rubbed at his left jaw as it always had when he was thinking. The action drew her eyes to his beard and the way his mouth moved beneath the neatly trimmed mustache. "What if they hunt eggs in teams instead of as individuals? Team versus team."

"Dr. Colter may be on to something," the teacher said. "My high schoolers will join anything if a competition is involved."

Claire frowned. "How would that work?"

"Here's my thought." Jake dropped both hands to the table and leaned forward, tapping his fingertips together as he spoke. "Teens gather their own groups of whatever number we decide, say six, and sign up as a team. Then, instead of a free-for-all race like the little kids, the hunt becomes a relay."

"That's brilliant, Dr. Colter." The teacher's face lit up with enthusiasm. "Each team member races to find an egg, brings it back to the basket, makes the tag, and then the next person goes. The first team to have all members finish wins."

"In order to include more kids, we could give prizes for three places." This from Mom. "And, win or lose, every team gets to divide the bounty inside their found eggs."

"I love this idea. It's perfect." The teacher tightened her ponytail as if excitement had loosened the band. "My classes will be thrilled. I can already imagine them gathering their teams."

Mom, who didn't seem to know when to keep quiet, piped up. "Rachel, since you're the chair and this is Jake's idea, why don't you two get together and figure out the particulars."

Seriously? Her own mother?

Swallowing the knot in her throat, she said, "I think Dr. Colter is probably too busy with work." He'd always been too busy with work, especially after they lost their baby. Work, work, work was all the man knew.

"Since he's taking Doc Howell's place on this committee, I'm sure he'll find time. Right, Jake?" Mom beamed at her ex-son-in-law.

Jake shifted in his chair, looking less than thrilled.

Good. She would not have to spend a single, awkward moment in his company. He'd refuse.

He didn't.

His eyes finding hers, he said, "Whatever the chairwoman thinks is best."

Rachel's belly sunk slowly to her feet.

Somedays she wondered if God was punishing her. Days like today.

Chapter Four

To Jake's relief, Rachel finally adjourned the meeting and attendees began to mill around, chatting and going for the refreshment table near the kitchen area.

Jake checked his cell phone for the time. This had been the longest meeting of his life.

First, he'd been assigned to Rachel's committee, where refusing would make him look like a jerk and cause him to get off to a bad start with half the town. He knew how the grapevine worked. Gossip would spread faster than an EF5 tornado that Dr. Colter refused to work with his ex-wife, who everyone knew was the nicest person ever.

Yeah. He'd fallen in love with her in high school because of her innate kindness and desire to help anyone in need. She never even complained about her extended family's neediness. Babysitter required for Aunt Sally's kids? Call Rachel. Granny needs a ride to the doctor an hour away? Call Rachel. A neighbor is sick or has a new baby or a lost job or had a bad hair day? Rachel is there with a casserole. Every time.

Funny that he'd remember those things today, when she'd stabbed him to death a hundred times with her eyes. Had she changed that much?

"Daddy, doughnut pwease?" Daley pointed hopefully toward the refreshment table and the candy-sprinkled pastries. His daughter was a sucker for anything with colored confetti on top. Or glitter.

Jake pushed his chair back and stood. "How about some strawberries instead?"

"Okay." Leaving her coloring book, she slid off the side of her seat and started toward the refreshments.

Jake followed.

One of the Myrick brothers clapped him on the back. "Great to have you back, Jake."

He paused to greet the old-time cowboy. "Thanks, Wink. I appreciate that. You still raising cows and horses?"

"Sure am. Doc Howell looks after 'em for me, but I reckon I'll be seeing you some now too." A little guy even in heeled boots and tall Stetson, Wink barely came up to Jake's chest.

His brother, Frank, in navy denim overalls to cover his considerable paunch, joined them. The two older men were mainstays in Rosemary Ridge. Or they had been twelve years ago before Jake left.

"We was sure proud when we heard you went to vet school. Takes some good smarts to do that." Frank rubbed a thick, wrinkled hand over the three sprouts of hair on his nearly bald head.

Jake grinned. "More hard work and effort than smarts, Frank, but thanks."

Talking to folks he'd known as a boy felt good, centered him. Getting reacquainted and rejoining the community was good for business, as well. Rachel might loathe him, but not everyone did. Even her mother had been friendly.

"That little 'un of yours sure is a cutie-pie." Wink pointed behind Jake. "She likes strawberries, don't she?"

Jake whipped around to find Daley piling a napkin with more fruit than she could possibly carry—or eat.

"Daley. Stop."

Big brown eyes blinked up at him. "Strawberries, Daddy. You said."

"Excuse me, Wink. Frank. Good talking to you, but I think my daughter needs attention."

Both men chuckled and moseyed over to talk with Sarah Ambruster.

As Jake assisted Daley, other townspeople paused to greet him, some asking advice about their animals and others simply welcoming him back to town.

He was feeling confident, eager to rejoin this town where he'd been raised when Rachel came toward him.

"Daddy, there's the nice wady."

Rachel was close enough to hear. "Hi, Daley. Did you like riding in the chief's car this morning?"

"Uh-huh. Moose too. He didn't bawk."

Rachel touched his daughter's head with what Jake saw as a wistful expression. "I'm glad you're safe."

"She sleepwalks." Jake felt a need to re-explain.

"So you said." The room temperature dropped ten degrees.

Jake cleared his throat. "About this committee thing."

One of her carefully arched eyebrows lifted. "Would you like to bow out? Be reassigned?"

"Is that what you want?" His chest began to burn inside. He hadn't had heartburn in months.

Her shoulders stiffened. Her lips formed a thin line. "You're the one who's always busy."

Here they went again. Seriously? After all this time? "You're the subcommittee chair, Rachel. If you want me out of the group, talk to Mrs. Ambruster."

"You know how well that would go. She's a barracuda

about changes. She sets up committees weeks in advance to make this event run smoothly, and any change upsets her balance."

"In other words, you're afraid to ask her to kick me off the committee, but you don't want to work with me." Her attitude hurt more than he'd expected. But then, he hadn't expected her negative attitude in the first place.

"The rest of us can do this without you. I'm sure you're very busy with the new job." Her words sounded polite but the meaning behind them was obvious.

"Dr. Howell asked me to take his place. I won't let him down. I'm sure you understand how important it is to please the new boss." His tone had grown tense. Enough that his conscience tapped at him. What would Jesus do in a circumstance like this?

Jesus never had an ex-wife, he thought with wry humor.

But he knew scripture well enough to know that God had an answer for every problem. In this case, the answer was the Golden Rule. Or maybe the love-your-enemies verse, except Rachel was never his enemy. She'd been his love, his life, until circumstances knocked them too far down to get back up.

He'd failed her. She'd failed him. They'd fallen apart.

Rachel tapped the toe of her ballet flats. Tension vibrated the air between them. She tilted her head toward the ceiling, took a deep breath and said, "Okay. I understand, but surely you agree this is an awkward situation."

"Only if we make it awkward."

She huffed. "You sound like my mother."

The Golden Rule, Colter. The one posted on the bulletin board when you were in first grade. Do unto others as you would have them do unto you.

Even if he didn't quite know how he wanted her to treat him. Civilly, at least. So he'd be civil to her.

"Your mom is a wise woman. What do you say we call a truce, work together in peace for the good of Easter and get this over with?"

A dozen conflicting emotions moved through Rachel's gray eyes, some of which he read quite well. Reluctance, worry, uncertainty, and finally, resignation.

"Can you take care of the teen egg relay yourself?" she asked.

"Nope. Don't know who to contact anymore."

She threw both hands up in frustration. "Really? This is how you cooperate?"

"Daddy?" Daley tugged on his pant leg. "Is the wady mad at us?"

Both he and Rachel turned toward his daughter, who watched them with wide, anxious eyes.

Rachel went to a crouch in front of his baby. His, not hers. "No, sugar, no. We're not mad."

She shot him a back-me-up glare.

"Miss Rachel and I are old friends, Daley. We're not mad."

At least, he wasn't.

"Okay. Can she come over and pway?"

This child. This child. She was sweeter than Grandma's Southern tea.

"Thank you, Daley, for asking, but I have a lot of work to do. And I'm sure your daddy is too busy for guests."

"Oh." Her little shoulders drooped.

Rachel felt about an inch tall. "Maybe another time, okay?"

What was she saying? She wasn't about to spend a minute inside Jake's house.

The bright little Daley perked up. "Okay. When? A-morrow?"

Jake rescued her. "Daley. Enough. Finish your strawberries. We need to go. On second thought, take them with you."

Rachel handed him an empty foam cup. "Take a few more. I think you like them."

Daley nodded her dark head. The sweet, soft curls bounced around her cheeks. She was a precious, beautiful little girl. Did Jake and his wife realize how fortunate they were?

"Say thank you," Jake urged.

"Thank you, Miss Wady." To her dad, she said, "I wike her. Don't you?"

Rachel tensed, waiting for the answer. None came.

Instead, he placed a hand against Daley's shoulder. "Get your jacket."

The child handed her dad the cup of strawberries and skipped toward the chair where she'd been sitting. The light fleece jacket was purple with a unicorn horn on the hood. Purple. Rachel was starting to see a pattern in Daley's clothing choices, even though her pants and sneakers were black.

A throb filled Rachel's throat, and as much as she grieved her own loss, she couldn't, wouldn't halt the compliment building inside.

"She's a lovely child, Jake." Was that an ache in her voice? "You and your wife have done a great job with her."

Jake's expression darkened. A scowl tugged at his forehead. He stared after his daughter before turning back to Rachel.

Voice gravelly, he said, "Her mother died."

Then, while Rachel reeled from the shock, he spun on his heel and walked away.

Chapter Five

"Did you know about his wife's death and didn't bother to tell me that either?"

Rachel settled on her mother's gray couch and squeezed the bridge of her nose. A headache threatened to ruin her evening. She had tons of committee work to do before Monday when she went back to her real job as office manager at the physical therapy clinic.

"I didn't, Rachel. Someone told me Jake was single but didn't mention he was a widower. That's sad."

"Very. He found happiness with another woman that he didn't find with me, had a beautiful child and then lost his wife. Even though *we* didn't work out, I never wanted him to suffer such an awful thing."

She felt terrible for bringing up the painful subject. Especially in front of that precious, *motherless* child.

"I know, honey. You'd never intentionally hurt anything. Remember how you used to scoop spiders onto a dust pan and take them outside so Dad wouldn't squash them?"

Rachel managed a smile. "Dad laughed at me."

"And indulged you."

"And you."

Mom's smile was tender. "Still does, when he's home."

After forty-five years, Mom and Dad still adored each other and missed one another whenever Dad was on the road.

Rachel wondered why she'd never found a love like theirs when she'd had such great examples of a solid marriage.

She rubbed her burning eyes. "I wonder what happened to Jake's wife."

Her mother tsked. "So sad. And his little girl motherless now."

Hadn't she been thinking the same thing? "Do you ever wonder why God takes people so young?"

"Of course. But I believe God is infinitely good and if we live for Him and trust in Him, He works all things for our benefit."

"I know you're right, but when awful things happen, I have trouble understanding." Awful things, like the loss of unborn children. Did other women grieve their pregnancy losses forever, the way she did?

Mom dipped around the corner into the small kitchen and returned with two cups.

"Some things have no earthly answers, Rachel. I pray, put the matter in His hands and keep moving."

She'd tried that, hadn't she? Yet she still had questions, even resentment. The agony of loss didn't go away no matter how silent the rest of the world was on the matter.

Mom must have read her expression. She was too good at that. Sue Ann Hamby had parental radar that could recognize sickness, headaches, stress and about any other kind of mood in a flash. Mom could tell her response to Rachel's question hadn't resolved anything.

"Faith, honey. We must have faith that He is Who He is and that His love and goodness is eternal." Mom set a cup of tea on the coffee table in front of her. "Drink this. Lemon balm is soothing. You're stressing."

"Thank you." Rachel leaned forward and breathed in the citrusy scent. The deep breath alone eased some of the tension gathering at the back of her neck.

She and Mom were both proponents of teas for a variety of issues. Mint for the stomach, echinacea for a cold, ginger for nausea. And good old Earl Grey for the doldrums.

After her foot-in-mouth moment with Jake, she needed lots of soothing tea.

"Did Jake say how long ago his wife died? Or how?"

"No, Mom. He didn't say anything. He walked off without a word. I'm sure the subject must be excruciating." She sipped the tea and grimaced. "Sugar, Mother. Sugar."

"Rots your teeth." Mom's singsong reminder was a familiar refrain. Sue Ann Hamby did not touch sweets.

Rachel wished she had her mom's willpower.

Since she didn't, she rolled her eyes and went into the kitchen for the sugar. Loving tea was one thing, but any brew tasted bitter without a sprinkle of something sweet. Mom had only honey, so with a sigh, Rachel used that.

"And," she said as she reentered the living room, "while I'm unloading on you, what were you thinking to suggest Jake and I work on the egg hunt together?"

Mom sipped her tea and shrugged, her eyes not meeting Rachel's. "Since he came up with the idea and you're the chair, I thought the two of you could put your heads together and make the event special."

"Too awkward, Mother, which is why I'm going to connect him with Sheila Ramirez. She'll know everyone at the high school and most of the teenagers. Sheila was the person eager to get the teenagers involved in the first place."

Mom sighed, a sure sign she thought Rachel was being unreasonable. "Whatever you think, dear."

Rachel pressed three fingers to her temple. "Got any pain reliever?"

"Are you getting another of your headaches?"

"Trying not to. I haven't had one in ages."

"That's good. Shane mentioned he might want you to watch the kids later while he and Kara go to a movie."

"My dear brother can text *me* if he wants something."

"Don't get testy. My, my, Jake Colter stirs a powerful reaction, doesn't he?"

"It's not him. It's—" *The other.* Except Jake was part of the other. She took a big drink of tea and rose. "I need to go home. Too much to do. See you tomorrow at church?"

With a purse of lips that said she knew Rachel was running away from the subject of Jacob Colter, her mom nodded. "Of course."

Rachel made her escape, hoping her brother wouldn't text her about the kids. She adored her two young nephews but she wanted to get rid of this headache and go right to work on organizing Easter.

In a small town, everything was close, so the drive across Rosemary Ridge took less than ten minutes. Five if she'd caught the town's single traffic light on green. Which she didn't.

As she turned her bronze Hyundai into her driveway, a big red dog trotted off her porch.

She frowned at the sight. Was that Jake's dog? Daley's dog?

After parking outside the garage, which was too full of storage to admit a vehicle, she circled the car, pinching her nose as she quickly scooted past the trash bin she'd forgotten to set on the curb yesterday.

"What are you doing here?" she said to the dog.

According to the brief conversation this morning with Jake and the chief, Jake had moved into the house directly behind hers. Moose, like his tiny owner, must have roamed across the alley and wound up here. Again.

The animal approached, plunked onto his bottom and lifted a paw.

Rachel shook it. "Aren't you the friendly one?"

His mouth opened, tongue lolling, golden eyes bright.

"Moose, isn't it?" She released the paw to rub her fingers over the long, soft mahogany-colored ears. "You're a pretty boy, aren't you?"

With a happily expectant expression, Moose lifted his paw again.

"All right, Moose. You've said hello." She gave his paw a shake and then gave the rest of his large frame a gentle push. "Go home now."

The dog didn't budge.

Giving up, she started toward the house. He followed.

"Shoo. Go home. Daley misses you."

At Daley's name, he barked a short yip.

"That's right. Daley. Now go." She waved her hands at him in a shooing motion.

He plopped his bottom on her shoe.

"You are a silly dog. What am I to do with you?" She wished she'd gotten Jake's phone number. As soon as the thought came, she squelched it. She did not want to see his name in her contact list.

Still, a phone call would be easier than forcing this overgrown puppy into her car.

Her neighbor across the street waved from his flower garden. The retired Norman Thacker and his wife Edna kept an eye on things up and down the block. Another reason Rachel didn't worry about unlocked doors. Norman was on duty. Always.

"Hi Norm." Rachel returned his wave.

He pointed a trowel toward Moose. "That dog's been on your porch all day. Is he yours?"

"No."

"Probably a stray. Call animal control."

Animal control? Daley would be heartbroken.

"No need," she called. "I know his owner. Come on, boy. I'll walk you home."

Norm went back to poking at his dirt while Rachel contemplated another meeting with her ex-husband.

She owed Jake an apology for her crude comment and Moose was as good an excuse as any.

"Daddy, daddy! The wady came to pway."

Jake interpreted his daughter's sentence as a lady coming to play or pray, but he still didn't understand the meaning. "What lady?"

They were in the kitchen. Jake was preparing dinner and Daley had her nose pressed against the glass patio door leading into the small backyard.

"And Moosey too."

Jake set aside the box of mac and cheese and joined his child at the glass door. He'd stopped at the grocery store long enough to grab the basics. Bachelor basics, he called them. Along with pigs in a blanket, mac and cheese and carrot sticks were his idea of a meal, especially when he still had moving boxes to unpack, including kitchen gear.

His back patio needed attention, too, but green grass had begun to overtake the dead brown of the small yard. A dappling of tiny purple-and-white wildflowers scattered along the strip of land dividing this side of the block from the other.

Strolling companionably across those hopeful little flowers were Moose and Rachel.

Jake's heart ricocheted against his chest wall. He couldn't tell if the sight of his ex-wife in his backyard was a thing of dread or pleasure. He and Rachel hadn't left today's Easter meeting on the friendliest of terms.

Her mention of Mallory had taken him aback. Caught him off guard. He'd reacted badly or, at best, oddly.

He rubbed a suddenly damp palm over his shirtfront.

They were neighbors. The Bible said to be at peace with everyone as much as possible. And he fully intended to be on friendly or at least peaceful terms with all his neighbors, including her. Rachel was the one with the grudge.

To a certain point, he understood her feelings. He'd failed her, failed them. But surely by now, she'd found a better guy than him and forgotten their past. At least, his part in it. He knew from painful experience that a parent never forgot the tragedy of losing a baby, even a preborn one.

Their world had stopped that day, even as the *rest* of the world continued onward. After that, nothing was ever the same again. Especially between him and Rachel.

Pushing the lock, he slid the door open. Daley barreled out and met Rachel and Moose halfway. He could hear her excited chatter but couldn't hear her words or those of Rachel.

The wind had shifted, the air cooled. "Are you lost?"

The breeze tickled the sides of Rachel's dark hair and brushed it away from her face. Gold hoops gleamed from her earlobes. Pretty.

"Your dog might be. He was in my yard when I got home." Her tone wasn't friendly but not rude either.

"Oh." His gaze dropped to Moose. Jake had gotten busy with dinner and forgotten to check on the dog's whereabouts. Hadn't he left Moose in the garage this morning? Apparently not. Some vet he was. "Thanks for bringing him home."

He needed to have a fence installed, but right now, he had more pressing things on his agenda. Like arranging day care, setting up his house, orienting with Doc.

Daley danced around Rachel's legs like a ballerina. Moose watched her with his usual happy expression.

Rachel took a few steps closer but stopped at the edge of his patio. She glanced toward him and then back to the dog, looking as discomfited as he felt. She didn't know what to say to him any more than he knew how to talk to her. But then, they'd not been able to communicate at all after the miscarriage. She'd spent her days in the nursery, crying over tiny baby clothes their son would never wear. Nothing he said or did penetrated her grief. Or his own. So he'd taken his anger and helplessness out on demolishing and rebuilding the backyard storage shed.

And the two of them had drifted apart.

There should be, he decided, a manual on how to cordially reconnect with an ex-spouse after years apart.

He crossed his arms and shoved his hands beneath his armpits. Part of him wanted to invite her inside. Should he? Or for once in his life, should he leave well enough alone? He couldn't fix things before. Why try now?

"About today's meeting," she said. "I'll send your contact info to Sheila Ramirez and the two of you can set up the teen event."

"Sheila who?" He lifted one eyebrow.

"The high school teacher."

Oh. In other words, Rachel refused to work with him any more than necessary. A likely indicator that she wouldn't want to enter his home.

"Fine. You're the boss." Did he sound terse? Harsh? He hadn't meant to, but he didn't know what to say or how to breach the chasm between them.

The vision of blue baby blankets in a never-used crib dangled between them, painful to recall.

Rachel's eyes flashed to his again. The gray depths had turned stormy, troubled. He'd always been able to read her eyes. He just hadn't been able to remove the pain he'd found there.

Today he saw confusion but something else too that made him wonder if she still suffered from the headaches that had begun after the miscarriage.

"Does your head hurt?"

She looked startled. "What?"

A weird question. He shouldn't have asked. Jake shook his head. "Nothing."

Daley slipped her hand into Rachel's as if they were old friends. Something about the pair of them standing in his backyard together made his heart pinch.

Two beautiful brunettes he'd loved with everything a man could give. For Rachel, what he'd given hadn't been enough. She'd pulled so far away from him he'd gotten lost in her grief. And in his own.

Definitely don't invite her inside.

"I owe you an apology."

Her words surprised him. He dropped his arms to his sides.

"For?" A heavy ache throbbed in his chest. Unexpected. Unwanted.

Rachel's expression darkened, stormier than before. A wrinkle appeared between her eyes. Yes. She had a headache.

"The last thing I said to you after the meeting. I didn't know. I'm sorry to bring up something that hurtful."

Still finding his hands oversize and useless, Jake shoved them into his back pockets. "Don't worry about it."

"Has it been...a long time? I mean, since it happened?" Again, she glanced at Daley as if choosing her words carefully for his child's sake. He appreciated the thoughtfulness. But then, Rachel had always been thoughtful of everyone. Mostly.

"Two years."

"Daley would have only been—"

"—fifteen months old." One minute he'd been a busy veterinarian focused on work, and in the next, he was a widower alone with a baby.

"That had to be hard."

Harder than she could know. Mallory had been a stay-at-home mother, responsible for Daley's care. After the plane crash, he'd been wild for a time, with grief and guilt and the sudden realization that he, and he alone, had a baby to raise.

"How did you manage?" she asked when he didn't continue the conversation.

He wouldn't admit that he hadn't managed too well, that he'd lain on the floor next to Daley's crib and cried out to God until he was hoarse. Without his faith and the knowledge that a barely walking baby depended on him to rise to the occasion, no matter how difficult, he might never have gotten up again. If not for his mom and his pastor, he wouldn't have.

"Mom came and stayed for a few weeks." Nowhere near long enough, but she'd helped him get his legs back under him and get moving again. His pastor had helped him deal with the losses, both that one and the one he'd left behind in Rosemary Ridge.

"Your mom's a good person."

Rachel and his parents had always been on friendly terms. The divorce had been hard on them too.

"Yeah. She is." Jake shifted from one chilly bare foot to the other, unsure what to say from here. Daley was too young to remember Mallory but old enough to be inquisitive. If they opened up a discussion of the plane crash and Mallory's death, she'd ask questions he wasn't prepared to answer.

"I should go." She pointed a thumb behind her.

"Right."

She hesitated as if she had more to say. "Okay."

The uncomfortable tension thickened. His shoulders tightened. "Come on, Daley. Dinnertime."

His toddler, who'd quietly picked a handful of purple flowers, was suddenly not quiet anymore. She leaped to her feet. Bits of grass and tiny petals scattered. "No! We didn't pway yet. Don't go."

Rachel went to a crouch in front of his daughter. She placed a hand on Daley's shoulder. "I'm sorry, honey. I really must get home. Maybe another time."

As in never.

Understanding that she was trying to make her escape without causing a temper tantrum, Jake stepped in. "You heard the lady, Daley. Another time."

He lifted his now-pouting daughter into his arms. Rachel was already walking away, her back to them.

His throat thickened. He longed to say something else, to somehow erase the awkwardness between them. Would she come inside and have mac and cheese with them if he asked? She'd always loved the cheesy noodles. Pigs in a blanket, not so much.

A longing for…something rose in his chest. Normalcy maybe. The need to erase the wrong he'd done to her. The pain they'd caused each other. His horrible failures. Nothing more.

She was halfway across the alley space, long hair blowing, dress swirling around her knees.

"Rachel," his mouth said before his brain engaged.

She turned her head and looked at him over one shoulder of the faded denim jacket.

A jumble of words formed in his head. He opened his

mouth. Closed it. Let the words fade. No use digging up bones.

"Thanks for bringing the dog home."

She tilted her head and walked onward toward a back patio very much like his, except hers was clean and organized into a tidy sitting area next to a small grill.

Jake watched until she reached the back door and disappeared behind the sliding glass.

He'd prayed about returning to Rosemary Ridge and believed the move was right for his daughter and their future. All he wanted was to raise his child in this bucolic small town less than thirty minutes from his parents, and someday, when the man retired, to buy Doc Howell's veterinarian practice. Roots. He wanted roots for his baby girl. And himself.

He had not expected to find his ex-wife living behind him. Nor had he expected to see her at every turn.

Would his heart eventually stop jumping each time they met?

Three times in one day. Was that a harbinger of things to come?

He thought he'd buried the emotions from their past, along with his feelings for her.

"Lord," he whispered, "what's going on here?"

Daley patted his cheek. "What, Daddy?"

"Nothing, baby. Nothing at all."

Chapter Six

The Howell Animal Clinic buzzed with activity. Monday mornings were busier than normal, since people inevitably waited until after the weekend to bring their concerns to the vet.

Jake pitched in to help, but until he got settled at home and found permanent childcare for Daley, he only worked until noon. Thankfully, Doc didn't object to having Daley in the clinic for now, and Mandy, the receptionist, kept her occupied when he was busy.

The arrangement wasn't ideal, but until he found adequate child care, this arrangement would have to do. Daley was his whole world. He wasn't about to leave her with strangers until they'd been thoroughly vetted. Another matter on his very long agenda this week.

"He'll mend quickly, Mrs. Sparkman." Having removed a fishhook from a Jack Russell puppy's paw, Jake handed the owner a packet of antibiotic with instructions for caring for the wound.

"Thank you, Doctor."

"Keep in mind that terrier pups are notorious mischief makers, so he may go right back to the garage in search of more adventure." He gave her smile. "Do both of you a favor and keep the fishing gear out of his reach. Okay?"

The woman's lips flattened. "I already gave Henry a piece of my mind for leaving his rod and reel in reach."

Jake had a feeling Henry would not forget again.

Mrs. Sparkman scooped the terrier off the exam table and clutched him to her chest. "Poor baby. Daddy didn't mean to hurt you. Nice Dr. Colter fixed you all up."

Making smoochy sounds while still consoling the wiggling pup, the woman left.

"Mr. Parsons is in exam two with his cat, Dr. Colter." The clinic's one vet assistant, Leah, spritzed the now-vacated metal table with antiseptic cleaner, her blond ponytail bobbing as she moved. "Doc's in surgery." She grimaced. "The other doc."

"I'll take a look."

Grabbing the folder from the tray outside exam two, he went into the next room.

"I'm Dr. Colter." He offered a hand to an elderly man holding an overweight calico.

"Parsons. Tom Parsons."

Mr. Parsons shook Jake's hand, though the action was tentative. "I usually see Doc Howell. Samantha's used to him."

"Doc is in surgery all morning. If you'd prefer to wait until this afternoon or come back tomorrow…" Jake let the thought drift.

"No, no. I guess if Doc hired you on, you must know what you're doing."

He'd encountered several comments like this and expected more. Doc Howell had treated the large and small animals of this area for so many years, pet owners hesitated to trust someone new.

Jake held his upturned fingers to the cat's nose. She

sniffed, her whiskers tickling his skin. Once he'd acclimated her to his scent, he scratched her ears. She turned her face into his hand and began to rub and purr.

"I'll take good care of her, Mr. Parsons. Now, let's have a look at this pretty kitty of yours."

The rest of the morning went similarly. More pet owners balked at seeing an unfamiliar vet but went away pleased. All except one.

When Jake later told Doc, his mentor said, "I never please her either, but she keeps coming back. Let's grab a coffee and unpack your morning while we have a chance."

The receptionist kept a full pot brewing.

"Let me check on Daley." Jake peeked around the corner toward the receptionist desk. "Hey, princess. Want to join Doc and me?"

Daley hopped to her feet, bringing her tablet, and followed him past the exam rooms and the door leading into the kennels.

Inside Doc's office, which could use some serious reorganization, Jake gave his boss a general breakdown of his patients and asked his opinion on the pygmy goat he'd treated for eating an Easter basket.

He'd no more than finished the discussion when Doc asked, "Speaking of Easter, how was the meeting Saturday?"

"Informative." Jake thumbed through a pile of brochures for everything from horse wormer to dog collars.

"Sounds about right," Doc chuckled, arms folded on top of his cluttered desk. The man was a great vet but not the best organizer. "Spring is already a busy time for us vets. I apologize for dumping more work on you, but I'm not up to any committees this year."

"No problem. You warned me when you hired me that the job would entail community service." Though he hadn't exactly thought community service would involve hiding colored eggs or relay races. He'd been thinking more along the lines of free spaying and neutering for the animal shelter. "The Easter committee is a good way to get reacquainted with the townspeople."

"Speaking of which, the clinic sets up a petting zoo at the Saturday egg hunt. I'll call local farmers and see who has baby rabbits and lambs to loan. Maybe tomorrow afternoon you and Daley can take a run out to the farms and check them over."

Interesting that Rachel had failed to mention the petting zoo during the meeting. Had that been on purpose, because of him? "Sure. Daley would love it."

Daley looked up from her ABCmouse game. "I loves bunnies. Daddy won't get me one."

Doc laughed. "Well, he might let you hold these and pet them. How would that work?"

"Can Miss Wady come, too? She wikes bunnies. She told me."

"Miss Lady?" Doc shot a curious look from Daley to Jake.

"Rachel Hamby."

"Rachel?" Doc's bushy eyebrows shot to his gray hairline. "Your ex—"

"Yes." Jake interrupted, shaking his head in warning. "She lives behind us."

"She bringed Moosey home," Daley said while poking a finger at her tablet screen. "She's nice."

"Yes, she is. One of the nicest women you'll ever meet, always helping someone else." Doc rubbed a thumb over his chin, his gaze thoughtful. "She never remarried, you know."

Jake gulped, surprised. Why hadn't Rachel remarried? They'd been young, in their midtwenties, when they divorced, and she was pretty and well-liked, a good person. Any man's dream wife.

Not that Rachel's history over the past twelve years was any of his concern.

"That chapter closed long ago, Doc."

"Some books are worth reading twice."

"Not this one."

Doc's eyebrows dipped low. "You still got hard feelings?"

He hadn't sorted his feelings for Rachel yet, but he was long over the anger. "None at all."

"Alrighty, then." Doc rolled back in his desk chair. "You shouldn't mind taking her along to see those animals for the petting zoo. She'd be good company and you've been gone a long time. Farmers may not remember you, but they know Rachel. And she knows them and where their farms are located. She'll help you get reacquainted, ease the way, so to speak."

Jake held his hands over Daley's ears and mouthed, "She's my ex, Doc."

When Daley tilted her face upward in question, he patted the top of her head and smiled.

"And you have no hard feelings. You just said so. I always wondered what happened between the two of you. Perfect match, everyone said. Daley likes her."

Jake didn't know what to say to such an outrageous suggestion, so he didn't say anything.

One thing for sure, he wouldn't ask Rachel to go along.

Even if he invited her, she wouldn't go.

Would she?

Chapter Seven

"You want me to do what?"

Rachel tugged the edges of her sweater closer, more
than stunned to have Jake Colter standing on her porch,
his usually tanned face as red as his dog's fur. His cute
little girl clung to his hand. Moose crowded protectively
against Daley's opposite side. Rachel didn't see a vehicle,
so the trio must have cut through the alley.

Jake scratched at his jaw and looked as excited about
this conversation as a kid in the principal's office.

"Daley wants you to go. Doc suggested it. Farmers
know you and I've been gone a long time."

In other words, Jake didn't want her along on these farm
expeditions but Daley and Doc had compelled him to ask.

Which was fine. She was equally compelled to refuse.

"Jake, I—" Rachel grappled for an excuse. It wasn't
in her nature to be mean. Their divorce had been mutual,
and though she'd been bereft, she'd never hated Jake. She'd
simply been too empty to go on.

He shifted onto his opposite foot. His Adam's apple
bobbed. "If you're too busy…"

There. An excuse. "I am."

She gazed up at the porch ceiling as if reading the laundry list of activities that would keep her hopping until bedtime. Most of them were phone calls at this point, which could be done anytime, but she didn't admit that. "Committee work for the town and some things for church. And my brother may need me to babysit."

Maybe. On Saturday. And this was Monday.

"Shane has kids now?"

She nodded. "Two boys."

"How old?"

Really? They were having a casual conversation about her nephews?

To make matters worse, some foolish part of her noticed the fatigue hanging on him like an oversize shirt. Fatigue and reluctance. He was tired, but Doc had asked him to do this errand. With her along. Jake Colter was the kind of person who wouldn't refuse no matter how tired he was.

Kind of like her.

If she thought about it, and to her consternation, she *was* thinking about it—him in particular—Jake had a lot on his plate. A move, a new job, a new home, a child to raise alone. And now, the added stress of the Easter egg hunt and trips to area farms to vet-check animals for the petting zoo.

She didn't want to feel sorry for him. In fact, she didn't want to feel anything for him.

But he was still Jake, the man she'd once loved.

"Five and seven. Aiden and Liam," she added, replying to his question about her nephews.

Her brain jumped in a half dozen directions. Remembering Jake and their past together was all jumbled together with her busy life today and the fact that Jake was back in town and now her neighbor.

"Shane's a good guy. I'm glad for him." Jake rolled his shoulders as if they ached. They probably did. His neck and shoulder muscles tended to bunch up when he was tired.

Or they used to.

She didn't mention that. And neither of them mentioned the friendship Jake had once shared with her brother or the hours of basketball they'd played together in her parents' backyard. She'd played a few games of Horse with them even after she and Jake married. They'd laughingly argued over every shot in those rowdy, fun games.

Such great times before they'd struggled to conceive and then miscarried the son she'd wanted so desperately.

She'd never asked Jake if he blamed her. She still wondered if he did. He had every reason to. *She* was the one who couldn't carry a child to term. *She* was the one who'd miscarried.

"Pwease, Miss Wady. They has bunnies. Daddy said."

The small childish voice drew her focus to Daley. She was a sweet girl whose big brown eyes could melt concrete. "Oh my. Bunnies, you say?"

The child had a single focus to visit the farms and she wanted Rachel along. Strange but endearing. Why had she chosen Rachel? Was it because Rachel had rescued her on the morning she'd gotten lost and wound up in a strange kitchen?

"Daddy will wet you pet them. Right, Daddy?"

Humor mixed with love filled Jake's expression. Tired eyes smiling, he said to Rachel, "If you're nice, I might even *wet* you hold one."

Rachel almost laughed. The teasing was exactly the kind of gentle humor Jake used during their years together.

But an outing with her? Why would he want that?

"I don't know, Jake. Is this really a good idea?"

Until last week, her life was going smoothly. No bumps. No ruffles. Though seldom a week went by that she didn't think of the family she didn't have, she lived a purposeful, productive life.

Her family and friends had advised her to get over the past and embrace the future. She thought she had.

Then suddenly, Jake Colter moved back to Rosemary Ridge and once again she had trouble sleeping, trouble focusing. Headaches. Anxiety slammed her at odd times as if something bad was about to happen.

She hadn't had an anxiety attack in years and didn't plan to start now.

She couldn't blame her emotional upheaval on Jake. The miscarriage was her fault. Yet, she blamed him for the breakup of their marriage.

Jake had stoically thrown himself into work and activities like tearing down and rebuilding the backyard shed. Clearly, he'd wanted to move on and ignore the loss of their son. If they didn't talk about it, it hadn't happened. Or so he seemed to believe.

Rachel had felt abandoned.

Even though she'd gone back to work and put on a smiling face, she'd fallen into a dark depression that lasted for months. He hadn't helped. The chasm between her and Jake widened with every moment of silence.

Friends and family who acknowledged the loss made comments that were more hurtful than helpful.

You're young. You'll have more babies. Those were the worst. She'd wanted *that* baby. Samuel Jacob Colter.

And they'd been wrong. She didn't have more babies. But Jake had.

Was that the reason he'd pushed past his own discomfort and invited her along on the farm trip? Because he'd do anything for his one living child?

She would have. If she'd had a child.

Anything. *Anything* for that baby.

As if reading her mind, Daley slipped away from her dad and approached Rachel, rock-melting brown eyes lifted to meet hers. She pulled the well-loved stuffed rabbit from behind her back and held it up.

"You can hold Mr. Bunny in the car. Pwease?"

With an inward sigh, Rachel knew she was about to agree to a miserable outing.

Except for Daley's occasional question from the back seat about bunny rabbits, the drive to the Fespermans' farm was silent. Not the comfortable quiet he'd once shared with Rachel, but a stiff silence fraught with emotions he could no more identify than he could erase the past between them.

He shouldn't have asked Rachel to come along.

Holding the steering wheel in a choke hold, Jake glanced toward her. She hugged the passenger door as if she might jump out.

Why had he capitulated to Daley's pleading? Did he feel guilty for taking her away from the familiar friends and neighbors in Tulsa? Or was he a weak, overindulgent dad inclined to give his child anything she wanted?

More importantly, why had his ex-wife suddenly become his daughter's latest obsession?

Miles of woods and grasslands dotted with a smattering of farmhouses passed in a blur. He tried to pay attention. He needed to know the lay of the land for future vet calls.

Over and over again, his thoughts strayed to the woman at his side. He racked his brain for neutral conversation—anything to break the aching silence—and came up empty. He was that tired. And she was that stiff.

Yet his thoughts centered on Rachel. What was she thinking right now? What had her life been for the last dozen years? Had she been happy? Why hadn't she remarried and had the family she'd wanted?

She was kind to Daley and Moose, cold to him. He

thought they'd parted with civility following the divorce. Did she loathe him that much?

Would he gain any ground and end the icy silence if he told her how sorry he was about everything that had happened?

Or would he make matters worse by bringing up the past?

He'd once known her so well. Now she confused him.

Jake glanced at his GPS and grimaced. No signal in these hills and woods.

He cleared his throat, swallowed hard. "Do you know exactly where the Fesperman farm is? The GPS quit on me."

Her head, turned toward the window as if she was fascinated with farmland, swiveled toward him. Expression empty, voice flat, she replied, "We're almost there. Take a left turn at the next section line."

"Thanks."

She turned back to the window and an open field.

Nothing much to see.

But she didn't want to look at him. Or talk to him.

Stress gathered the muscles across the back of his shoulders.

The tension inside the truck cab stretched tighter than a good, strong suture.

He hunched his shoulders, rotated his neck and heard the crackle and pop.

The sound jogged a memory—Rachel laughing at his noisy neck as she massaged his stiff, cracking muscles.

Did she ever think of the good times?

Maybe he should start talking about his day and see if that helped. He could tell her about the pet squirrel he'd treated and the newborn colt that was born after the rainstorm on Sunday with a lightning mark on his forehead.

Would she be interested?

Jake glanced her way and back to the road.

By the stiffness of her body, he didn't think so.

He held in a sigh as he made the turn at the corner and soon came to a small, tidy farm he hoped was the Fesperman place.

"This is it," Rachel said and was out of the truck before he could kill the engine.

Daley's car seat was on his side of the truck. He helped her out and caught up with Rachel's purposeful stride.

A robust, middle-aged woman in heavy work boots, jeans and a man's red plaid shirt over a white T-shirt met them in the yard beneath a huge oak tree. If Jake had ever met her, he didn't remember.

"I'm Becky Fesperman." She stuck out a hand and gave a hearty shake. "Doc Howell called. You the new vet?" She eyed his dually truck with approval. A country vet required a heavy-duty vehicle.

"Yes, ma'am. Jake Colter." Beside him, Daley danced with excitement. He motioned to her. "This little bouncer is my daughter, Daley."

The rough, weathered skin around Becky's eyes crinkled. "Hello, Daley. Are you here to see my rabbits?"

Eyes bigger than saucers, Daley nodded eagerly.

Jake turned toward Rachel. "And this is my—" Uh-oh.

"Neighbor," Rachel put in with a smile toward the woman. "Becky and I know each other. How are you, Becky?"

Heat suffused Jake's face at his near miss. He couldn't help but admire the smooth way Rachel had saved him from major embarrassment. How did one introduce one's ex-wife to a client, anyway?

Mrs. Fesperman waved toward an area of outbuildings to the left of the white farmhouse. "The rabbit hutches are attached to the barn. Come on and I'll show you. The bunnies are out for their evening play right now, so this is a good time. Doc says you're doing an Easter petting zoo again this year. Any of my babies will work for that if you find them fit and healthy. They are as tame as kittens."

"Great. Let's have a look." Jake walked alongside the woman, listening as she discussed the care and health of her rabbits.

Daley clung to Rachel's hand and alternated between hops and skips as they made their way to the barn. With a soft smile, Rachel let her bounce along.

He appreciated Rachel's simple little bit of kindness and attention toward his child. *There* was the Rachel he knew.

Attached to the barn, a row of rabbit hutches was surrounded completely by narrow mesh wire divided down the center. A lop-eared breed hopped and played on one side while snowy white, straight-eared bunnies occupied the other.

"Lops and American?" he asked.

The woman offered an approving look. "Mini Lops, and yes, American, the classic Easter bunny. You know your rabbits." She patted the arm of his jacket. "We're going to get along fine, I think."

He wished he could say the same for Rachel and him.

"Bunnies!" Daley squealed with delight and hopped three times, her hands squeezed tight against her chest. "I'm a bunny too."

Mrs. Fesperman laughed. "I feel the same way every time I come out here, Daley."

"Beautiful animals, Mrs. Fesperman," Jake said. The enclosure was clean, spacious and provided over and above the basic needs for healthy rabbits.

"Thank you. I have my sweet bunnies. Ed has his cantankerous cows. My bunnies are easier because I don't have to hunt for them when they're having babies. Like Ed is doing right now."

Grinning, the friendly woman unlatched the gate leading into the lop enclosure.

"The Easter committee appreciates your willingness to bring your bunnies for the petting zoo, Becky," Rachel said. She kept one hand on Daley's back as they entered the enclosure. "Not everyone likes the idea of excited children handling their livestock."

Becky waved her off. "I'll be there to supervise, but I've never had a problem with children handling my bunnies. I take time to teach the proper way. How will they learn to respect and enjoy animals if they never have a chance to interact?" She raised both eyebrows and grinned. "Besides, the petting zoo is a good advertisement for my business."

Jake watched the Mini Lops explore their environment. Several stopped to eye the newcomers with interest and twitching noses. A larger gray hopped within reach. Bending low, he stroked the soft fur. The rabbit pressed its chin to the grass and closed its eyes.

Mrs. Fesperman noticed and said, "For a petting zoo, I usually recommend the lops since they are smaller. The Americans make great pets too. I sell a lot to school kids for fairs and shows, so I spend plenty of time with them to be sure they're ultratame before they go to new homes. My grandkids help out with that too. That's Watson. He's a friendly boy who loves forehead scratches."

Aware that his daughter was about to levitate with excitement, Jake went to one knee and pulled Daley to his chest. It wouldn't do to have a three-year-old running around the pen, chasing rabbits.

Rachel stood next to him, watching the rabbit and Daley. Her knee brushed his shoulder. The subtle fragrance of her floral perfume wafted past the scents of spring and rabbits.

Hyperawareness flooded through Jake. Did Rachel realize how close she was? Or was she too enraptured of his daughter's reaction to the rabbits that she didn't notice?

He certainly did.

"I want him. Pwease, Daddy."

Grateful for the interruption of a thought path he'd better not take, Jake forced a chuckle. His daughter wanted every animal she saw and thought *please* was the word that unlocked every door. Usually it was. "Sorry, princess pea. We have Moose. He's enough."

"Your little one can hold Watson if you say it's all right." Mrs. Fesperman waited until Jake nodded before she crouched in front of his daughter and gathered Watson into her arms. "He's a Mini Lop who loves gentle cuddles. Here's how you hold him." She displayed the proper form. "Can you do that?"

"Yes. Daddy showed me at the office. When anmals be sick, I be verrry gentle."

"Do you like his long ears? We call them lop ears."

"He's pretty. I wike him bunches."

"Tell you what. Why don't you and Rachel play with Watson while your daddy gives the others a checkup? If that's okay with your dad."

"Sound like a reasonable plan." He glanced up at Rachel. Their eyes met. Something stirred. In him? In her? Somewhere. "Rachel?"

"Fine." As if realizing she stood too close, Rachel took the rabbit and stepped back. She held the bunny under one arm and stroked a hand over Daley's baby-soft curls with the other. Tender, loving. As a mother would.

A yearning took him by surprise and curled inside him like a hunger he couldn't assuage.

"Come on, precious. I see a good sitting spot right over there on that straw."

Precious. In the kindest, sweetest voice, as if the word came from her heart, she'd called his daughter precious.

The tug to know Rachel again grew stronger.

To get his unexpected emotions under control, Jake watched for a minute while Rachel and his daughter settled with the rabbit. *His* daughter, not hers.

He needed to keep that in mind.

Straightening his shoulders, he continued through the enclosure with Mrs. Fesperman, lifting first one rabbit and then another, checking teeth, listening to the rapid heartbeats. All seemed healthy.

"Doc and I will clip nails for you and neuter any you choose before Easter. Like Rachel said, the Easter committee appreciates your service."

"I can't argue with a deal like that."

While he and Mrs. Fesperman chatted, Jake kept an eye and ear tuned to his daughter. She sat cross-legged in front of Rachel on a pile of fresh straw with Watson, the bunny, between them on the ground. He relished Daley's giggle and Rachel's accompanying laugh.

Beautiful sounds.

His heart squeezed.

Rachel was good with his daughter.

She just didn't like him.

The knowledge shouldn't hurt anymore. But it did.

Chapter Eight

Days passed. Rachel, her schedule full, finally stopped thinking about the outing with Jake and Daley. A few hours of discomfort hadn't killed her. They'd accomplished their goal of securing healthy bunnies for the Easter petting zoo. Jake mentioned something about finding lambs, too, but he hadn't invited her. Thankfully.

She'd actually enjoyed her time with Daley. Such a darling little girl. Her reaction to the rabbits was priceless, so Rachel hadn't objected when Jake pointed his phone camera in their direction. The fact that he wanted to capture his child's life on video touched her, and she wondered if he'd have done the same for their child. Had their loss made him more attuned to the precious gift that a child is?

When the farm visit ended, Rachel had been relieved to put the pair out of her thoughts. Mostly.

That is, until she walked into the family center of South Cross Church to help with the church's Easter pageant. As the unofficial costume designer, Rachel had been known to sew as many as ten costumes in one very long night. She'd like to avoid that this year.

Children buzzed around the open, all-purpose space, chattering like happy squirrels. The dozen adults already in attendance attempted to organize them into groups. The smell of fresh coffee permeated the air, though tea bags and hot water were available too. Ready for a cup of soothing tea after a busy day at the office, Rachel headed toward the drink table.

"What's this year's plan?" Still jiggling her car keys, Rachel filled her cup next to the pastor's wife. Farah Everly, whose silver-blond hair was never out of place, pushed up her red-framed glasses. She was a pretty, stylish, slightly round woman only a few years older than Rachel. She served in the pastorate alongside her husband, teaching Bible, running the women's group, and about any other pastoral duty needed.

"Palm Sunday belongs to the littles. With the help of a few adults, they'll act out Jesus's entry into Jerusalem, which leads the congregation into a time of worship and praise."

"Similar to last year?"

"Exactly. Claire and your mother have already procured the palm branches. Our usual director, Abby Potter, will assign parts tonight and start practice."

"What about costumes?"

"That's where I need you." Farah gestured toward the end of the gym floor. "Will you look inside the storage room and find them, check to see if they're in good shape, and do whatever is needed to make them workable? You know better than me. I can't sew a single stitch."

"You don't need to. You're the master organizer."

Farah laughed. "As Pastor's wife, taking charge is kind of a given, but I'm very thankful for volunteers like you who don't need direction. You take the ball and run."

"I'm happy to serve the church in any way I can. You know that."

"I do." Farah patted Rachel's forearm. "Now, before you

head to the storeroom, let me see if your assistant is here yet. He claims he can sew."

"He?" A male seamstress? That was different. And rather cool. A nice change. Most years, her assistant was a girl student from the local sewing class, but boys, she knew, sometimes took the class too.

"He's new but says he attended South Cross years ago before Bill and I were pastors." Farah stretched up on tiptoes. "There he is. I'll grab him right quick and introduce you."

New in town? Attended South Cross years ago?

Rachel's feet seemed nailed to the floor. Foreboding tugged through her midsection. This couldn't happen again. Could it?

It could.

Near the entryway and in Rachel's line of sight, Farah hooked her arm around Jake Colter's elbow. With an animated smile and talking a mile a minute, the pastor's wife threaded her way and his through the gaggle of excited children.

When she stopped in front of a stunned Rachel, Jake stared for a minute before shaking his head. "No way."

"What?" Farah's smile turned to concern. "Is something wrong? Do you two know each other?"

The current pastors had only been in Rosemary Ridge eight years. Farah had no idea what she'd stepped in.

"No worries, ma'am." Jake turned his charming smile on Farah. "Everything is fine. Rachel and I go way back."

Right, Rachel thought. Way, way back. Which meant she should be over this shaky reaction, over the sudden clutch in her chest anytime she thought of their shared past. She should be, but she wasn't.

Lord, why can't I move on like everyone says I should? Jake did. My life is full and blessed, so why does seeing Jake make me feel that my world is collapsing all over again?

She set her cup aside and forced a pleasant expression.

Easter was her favorite holiday, but this year, she couldn't wait until the day was over.

"Can I ask you something?"

Inside the storage room in a building that hadn't been here twelve years ago, Jake pushed aside a box of Christmas lights and contemplated his ex-wife. Rachel had said little, but she was as stiff as the cardboard donkey propped against one wall.

A black plastic bag crinkled as she opened it and peered inside. "Depends."

"I need your opinion."

She glanced up, curious. "Okay. What is it?"

"Do you think there have been one too many coincidences going on around here?"

Her forehead puckered. "What do you mean?"

"Think about it. We're assigned to the same Easter egg committee, then Doc practically forces me to take you to the Fesperman farm, which you hated, and now we're working together on church pageant costumes? Doesn't that seem a little too suspicious to you?"

Rachel stopped digging in the bag and stared at him. "Doc forced you to take me along?"

"Let's say he strongly suggested, and as the new guy, I couldn't turn him down. Same thing tonight. The pastor called and asked if I could sew, being a vet and all. Weird question, huh?"

Pulling out a disciple's brown robe, she sat back on her heels. "I hadn't noticed before, but now I see what you mean."

"Do you smell a conspiracy?"

"As if someone is trying to force us together?"

"Yeah. *Yeah.*" One eye squinted, he scratched the side of his short beard. "Maybe."

"As in *matchmaking*?" Her expression widened, incredulous, maybe a tad horrified. "Between us?"

He hitched a shoulder and waited, thinking exactly that.

Rachel's dark hair swished back and forth on her shoulders as she disagreed. "That's impossible. Our friends and family know we divorced. You've remarried, had a child."

Except they were both single now.

He lifted both hands. "No argument here." She didn't have to sound *that* appalled. "But still, I'm suspicious."

Rachel's mouth flattened. She glanced down at the disciple's costume as if searching for answers in the brown fabric. Finally, she huffed once in utter disgust and asked, "How do we stop them?"

"I don't know." He bent back the flaps on a cardboard box marked Props. "We're not even sure it's happening. Maybe the fact that we keep running into each other really *is* coincidental."

She ran her fingers along the seams of the robe, but her focus was on him. He kind of liked that.

"When did you start believing in coincidence?"

"Never." That she recalled this minutia pleased him. "God's the director of my path, not chance."

"So you're saying God is bringing us together?"

Would that be so terrible? If God gave him an opportunity to mend fences, to make up to her for what he couldn't fix back then?

Jake sighed. Apparently, she thought so.

In spite of the ache beneath his breastbone, he managed a short laugh. "Rachel, I don't know what's going on. More likely some well-intentioned old friend noticed we're both single again and pulled some strings."

"If that's the case, I don't understand their reasoning."

Like a well-aimed dagger, the comment stabbed him in the chest.

Going silent, Jake turned his attention to the jumble of items in the prop box.

As a boy, he'd considered Easter all about colored eggs and prizes, and while he wanted the fun memories for his daughter, he'd come to appreciate the real meaning behind Easter. Daley already knew that Jesus loved her and she should follow Him with her life. The difficult subjects of Jesus's death, burial and resurrection would come as she grew older. But they would come. Daley would know her Redeemer. As he did.

They opened the lids to a few more boxes and found several useful costumes and props. After rummaging for glue, paint and other supplies, Jake started work on the items that needed repair.

Taking the costume box to examine the garments for tears or missing buttons, Rachel moved to the opposite side of the room. As far away from him as possible.

Was she trying to escape him? He wasn't Jack the Ripper. Yes, they'd hurt each other, but they'd parted in kindness. At least, he believed they had.

"Rachel."

"What?" She looked as eager for conversation as if he'd ask her to drink poison.

"Do you think I'm a terrible person?"

"What?" Her forehead furrowed. "No. Of course not. I never thought any such thing."

"Back then, I wondered," he said softly, "and since returning to Rosemary Ridge, I still wonder if you hate me."

"We're both Christians, Jake. We can't hate each other. Do you hate me?"

"Never. Not for one moment. I couldn't. No matter what we went through, I never hated you." *I loved you with everything I had and it wasn't enough.*

Across the cluttered storeroom, they shared an aching moment as memories hovered between them.

"Okay," she said and dropped her gaze to the garment in her hands.

Jake waited one long minute to see if she'd say anything else. When she didn't, he murmured, "Okay."

Some things were better left alone. No matter how much he wanted to fix the hurt, or at the least, to be friends again, he still couldn't. She wouldn't let him.

Maybe some things were unfixable.

Jake's question and the pain in his eyes bothered Rachel for days afterward. They'd worked together on the costumes and had even had a laugh or two over Jake's shockingly accomplished sewing skills, due, he claimed, to suturing animals on a regular basis. But the tension in the air remained, as if both of them were fragile glass the other could break.

She didn't want to hurt Jake. She had never wanted to cause him pain and deeply regretted her part in their breakup. Their faith strongly discouraged divorce for reasons she'd come to understand all too well. The hurt, the failure, the guilt never ceased.

Many times she'd prayed for forgiveness. She'd even prayed for Jake.

But she never wanted to suffer like that again either. The damage had been too great.

She could not, however, get Jake's questions, or him, off her mind. Everyone who entered the physical therapist's clinic stirred up thoughts of Jake. They were either excited about the upcoming Easter events or the nice new veterinarian.

As she arrived home from work one windy evening, Moose grinned from her front porch.

"You again?" She slammed the Hyundai door and started across the grass. Moose rose, rattled his dog tags with a hard shake and trotted over to meet her.

She rubbed his silky red ears and wondered why she'd never gotten a pet. She'd once considered a cat but didn't want to become known as the weird, old-maid cat lady. Plus, she was gone entirely too much with church, civic and work duties. She couldn't spend adequate time with an animal.

"Come on, boy. I'll walk you to the alley. Then you are on your own."

She should have known better. When they got to the alley, fighting the wind all the way, Rachel started to turn back toward her townhouse. Moose turned back with her and whined.

With a loud huff to let him know he was a nuisance, Rachel crossed the expanse of tiny purple-and-white wild-flowers leading to Jake's back patio. He really needed to clean this up. A broken lawn chair had blown onto the grass. Spider nests and webs gathered in the corners over leaves from last fall. The brown leaves crunched as she stepped up on the concrete and tapped against the patio door.

A heavy turquoise drape covered the glass. She couldn't see inside but she heard the clatter of pans. The scent of cooking food seeped through the door.

Moose whined. Rachel's belly grumbled. She frowned. Had she skipped lunch again?

Tempted to knock hard and then hurry away like some kid on a dare, she pointed a finger at Moose. "Stay."

As she started to brave the wind again, the sliding door scraped open.

"Rachel?" Jake's gaze fell to Moose. "Again?"

Rachel nodded and slid her fingers along the top of

Moose's soft, wide head. He really was a charming dog. "He was on my porch when I got home from work."

"Sorry." Jake raked a hand wearily through his hair. "I have to get a fence put up but—" He blew out a gusty breath and made a face.

"Too busy?"

"Yeah, every day has been wild since we got here. Half our belongings are still packed in boxes in the garage. I can't even find the sheets for Daley's bed."

He'd been here this long and still wasn't unpacked?

Despite her thoughts of a quick escape, she asked, "What's she sleeping on?"

"King-size sheets wrapped around her twin mattress several times?" An appealing grin peaked from beneath his mustache. Endearing. Familiar.

Leave, Rachel. Go home.

"You'll get there," she said instead. "Setting up a new home takes time. I've lived in my townhouse for three years and still don't know what happened to my Bundt pan."

Eyebrows dipped low in a comical scowl, Jake scratched at his jaw. "I don't even know what that is. If I have one, I can't find it."

In spite of her reservations, Rachel chuckled.

"So, hey," he said and stepped to one side, "come on in. You're about to blow away. Moose, you too, you scoundrel."

"Oh no. Thanks, but I got home from work only a few minutes ago."

"Then, you haven't had dinner."

"No, but—"

Jake heaved a heavy sigh and leaned a broad shoulder against his opened glass door. Defeat. And fatigue.

Yet, he was being cordial in the face of her intentional resistance.

Shame heated her cheeks. From the first meeting of the Easter committee, she'd behaved rudely but Jake hadn't.

Daley peeked from behind his knees. "Miss Wady!"

"Hi sweetie. I brought your dog home."

"He wikes you." Daley patted the chest of a pink sweatshirt. "I too."

"Well, thank you. I like you too."

"Does you wike pasgetti?"

"Spaghetti," Jake clarified. "Yes, Daley, she does."

The fact that he remembered stirred in Rachel. "So does your dad. Spaghetti is a favorite."

"For both of us."

Rachel flashed a look at Jake. "Yes."

A beat, then two, pulsed between them. She'd known all his favorites and he'd known hers.

Thoughtful dark eyes studied her with something akin to hope. "Come on, Rachel. It's only spaghetti."

Except it wasn't.

Her heart thumped a couple of times, hard. Should she? Was she opening a door she didn't want to look behind? A door to heartache?

He was her neighbor. That's all. A man she used to know. If she could think of him in that manner, she'd be fine. After all, the Bible said to treat your neighbors well.

She refused to mentally quote the commandment to love thy neighbor. She wasn't going that far. But she was not normally unkind, and she'd struggled since the first committee meeting with guilt over her rude behavior toward him.

If she didn't hate him, as she'd claimed at the church, she needed to prove it.

To save face, she said, "Do you have garlic bread? You can't have spaghetti without garlic bread."

One side of his mouth twitched. "Is Rome in Italy?"

Which meant he had garlic bread.

Rachel snorted. "Last time I checked which might have been in a high school geography class."

"Eleventh grade. Mr. Philbrook."

"He looked like Einstein." She held her hands to the sides of her head to indicate the man's fuzzy white hair.

Jake laughed. "Yeah. He did. He was a good teacher. I can still find all the rivers of North America on a map."

"Me too."

The wind grabbed a handful of leaves and swirled them up between her and Jake. She shielded her eyes, coughed.

Jake batted at the leaves.

"So, stay and eat. No leaves or wind inside. I'll drag out the atlas and challenge you to a geography quiz. What do you say?" He pushed the door wider.

Rachel was tempted, and not because of the menu. Or the wind.

While she wrestled with indecision, Daley slipped from behind her dad to take Rachel's hand. "Want to see my toys? Come on."

Such a small thing and such a small child to wield such power.

It couldn't be the dad.

"How can I pass up a deal like that?"

Jake felt as if he'd won the Nobel Prize for Animal Medicine, if there was such a thing.

He badly wanted to bridge the divide between Rachel and him, though he couldn't say exactly why, other than they'd once been best friends as well as husband and wife. They'd planned a future together.

Since moving back to Rosemary Ridge, he'd thought about those plans and about Rachel more than he had in years. Natural, he supposed, all things considered. They were on the same Easter and church committee. She lived behind him. His dog and daughter seemed enamored of her. Every time he took Daley out in the backyard to play, she gazed longingly toward Rachel's patio and wanted to go over there.

So far, he'd resisted. Today Rachel had come to him. Rather, Moose had brought her.

He didn't know whether to be pleased that his dog wouldn't stay in his own yard or annoyed.

Since tonight was spaghetti night and Moose had coerced Rachel to cross the grassy divide in the miserable March wind, Jake chose pleased. Negative feelings caused indigestion. Especially with garlic involved.

"Smells good." Rachel stood inside the door, surveying his cluttered kitchen-dining room combination. "Your house is similar to mine. Different finishes but otherwise the same layout."

Jake's kitchen ran along the left wall with the fridge to the right of his stove and a small island centering the room. A table and chairs lined the right wall. The kitchen-dining combo extended into a small living space with a staircase at the entryway and a garage door next to it.

"Most of the townhouses in this neighborhood appear to have been built by the same builder."

"Yes. I suppose."

He couldn't say Rachel looked relaxed, but she didn't seem intent on bolting either. Not like the trip to the farm.

"Sorry for the clutter." He knew her as an immaculate housekeeper. Though not grumpy about tidiness, the artsy Rachel had a place for everything and everything in its place. She'd even created a special organizer for his baseball hat collection. He still used it. Well, he would when he could find it. He'd had little time to unpack.

As if the clutter didn't bother her, Rachel shrugged off his apology. "Need any help?"

"With dinner or with the clutter?"

Her eyes cut to him. A warning maybe not to push too hard. She wasn't ready for his weird humor.

"Dinner. I could make a salad."

He winced. "Not happening."

"Tsk-tsk. Veggie hater."

"I'm better than I once was." He tipped his chin toward his daughter, who'd left and now reentered the room with an armful of toys. "I'm trying to set a better example. I want her to eat well. Can you believe she likes radishes? And broccoli?"

"Smart girl. Do you have either of those?"

He stirred a savory-scented pot of sauce. Steam rose toward the overhead exhaust fan. "Yeah. Yeah. I think. Maybe."

Rachel shook her head as if she thought he was hopeless.

He wasn't, but he'd had very little time to worry about groceries. He'd grabbed a few things here and there but had yet to go on a major shopping expedition. He'd planned one a few times but something always came up.

"I'll look." Rachel started toward his fridge and then hesitated. "If that's okay with you. This isn't my house."

A charge shot between them. Jake was not about to address it. Whatever *it* was.

"Make yourself comfortable." Not that he expected her to.

He started to add *"Mi casa es su casa"* but held back the common phrase people used to show hospitality. Neither needed the reminder that they'd once lived in the same home. The mention of their shared history would send her out the door faster than he could give an injection. Which was really fast.

Rachel poked around in his fridge and came out with a bag of radishes and a box of cherry tomatoes but no broccoli.

"Nothing green, Jake. You and Daley need green."

"Yeah, yeah." He waved a wooden spoon over the boiling pot. "I'll get right on it."

She rolled her eyes at him and opened an overhead cabinet. The shelves were empty.

"Plates? Saucers? Anything to put these on?"

"Mmm." Frowning, he laid aside the spoon and rustled through a cardboard box beside the island. "I guess we used the first pack of paper plates, but I should have more somewhere. Real plates too. I'm not sure where they—"

"—are," she said, a mini reminder of the way they'd once finished one another's sentences. Even each other's thoughts.

"Right. However—" he intentionally elevated his tone to sound like a prize announcer on a game show "—I have...*this*."

With a dramatic flourish, he whipped out a plastic Frisbee. "Ta-da! A serving platter."

Rachel pressed her lips together. Her eyes widened, sparkled. She curled inward and laughed.

Grinning, Jake watched her, pleased that his silly joke had brought about the change. From tense and cautious to an all-out laugh displayed her beauty in a way nothing else did. He'd always admired that about her. Her joy.

After the baby loss, she'd become sad and depressed. No joy in anything. Not even him. Especially not in him.

He hoped her laughter was a sign that she'd found joy again.

She deserved that.

He wanted her to be happy.

When she finally stopped laughing and wiped her eyes, she plopped out a hand. "Give me that Frisbee."

In his best pitching form, Jake pulled back his arm and gave the toy an easy fling.

Rachel dipped to one side and let the disc clatter against the far wall.

"You were supposed to catch it. Moose does."

Rachel gave him another you're-hopeless look, which kind of tickled him. Tonight, she was interacting instead of giving him the stony freeze-out.

With a shake of her head and what he thought might be a tiny grin, she picked up the Frisbee and carried it to the sink where she scrubbed the plastic clean.

"A serving platter, it shall be."

There she was. Rachel. The Rachel he'd once loved.

Not that he had any such misguided notions these days.

With raising Daley and growing a busy animal practice, he had no time for romance. Besides, a man who'd drowned twice wasn't eager to get back in the ocean. Two strikes and he was out for good. And any other fitting metaphor. Even though Mallory had died before they could part, both had known they were headed in that direction.

"Necessity is the mother of invention." He ripped off a paper towel.

She took the towel and dried the Frisbee. "I smell something. Are you burning the garlic bread?"

"No. Oh. Yes." Rushing to the stove, he ripped open the oven and yanked out the foil-wrapped package with his bare hand.

"Ouch, ouch, ouch." He shook his fingers before sticking them under the cold water. "Daley, don't ever do that."

Daley, intent on stacking colorful, bug-eyed Jenga

blocks on top of each other, looked up from the table. "Do what, Daddy?"

"Touch something from a hot stove."

With a nonchalant "Okay," she went back to her blocks.

While he nursed his scorched fingertips, an ice cube appeared before his eyes.

"Hold this. I'll take care of dinner."

"Before I ruin it?"

She smirked. "I wasn't going to say that."

His index finger practically sizzled with relief from the ice cube. The rest of his skin sizzled with something entirely different.

Might as well admit it. Rachel Hamby still affected him in ways he hadn't expected.

Chapter Nine

Recover Physical Therapy was the kind of comfortable, hometown business that made working there easy, even on their busiest days. Rachel loved her receptionist/office manager's job and the clients who came and went.

"Good to see you feeling better, Whitney," she said to the teenager on her way out. "Was this your last PT session?"

"Sure was." The high school student, a star softball pitcher, rotated her shoulder. "Kim cleared me to work out with the team again. I'm stronger than ever."

"Great. Stay well."

With a wave and a smile, the ponytailed girl exited the building.

Rachel's boss and co-owner of Recover PT stepped around the corner from the gym area to relinquish Whitney's completed chart.

"That's the best part of my job." Rachel motioned to the departing young student. "They arrive in pain and walk out with a smile, all better."

Kim took the next client's chart from the plastic bin Rachel kept ready. "My favorite part too. Sometimes the effort takes a while, but I like to think we make a difference in every single patient." She cast a smile toward the waiting client. "Right, Mr. Jameson?"

"Yes, ma'am. I'm better every time." He winked toward Rachel. "Even when she tortures me."

Laughing and chatting amiably, the athletic Kim led the man into the gym.

The door opened and Rachel glanced up, expecting to greet the next client. Instead, Sarah Ambruster marched inside.

Without preliminary, she clunked her oversize purse onto the counter and announced, "Rachel, we have a problem."

"We do?" Rachel slid Whitney's completed client chart next to her computer for data entry and insurance filing. "What's happened?"

"James Redchief, the artist who volunteered to paint Easter murals on all the businesses?"

"Yes. What about him? Don't tell me he changed his mind this late in the game."

Sarah's head dropped back as if she was beseeching heaven. "His body changed it for him. He's in the hospital, facing surgery and a long recovery."

"Oh no. I'll pray for him."

"I'm sure he'll appreciate the sentiment, as do I, but I need someone to paint those murals. Now. They should already have gone up. Why, this town looks like we have no interest in Easter at all, much less a seventy-fifth anniversary. A crying shame, I tell you, and the lack reflects on my leadership."

Mrs. Ambruster took her leadership role very seriously. Anyone who didn't snap to attention heard about their lacking, loud and clear.

"I'm sure no one will blame you for someone's illness."

"Oh yes, they will. I should have had backup or, at the least, someone to coax businesses into decorating for themselves. You'd think these store owners were helpless. After my visit yesterday, the gift shop finally stuck a bucket of tulips and a basket of colored eggs outside their doorway, but otherwise, downtown Rosemary Ridge is practically bare." She thumped the side of her fist on Rachel's counter. "We have got to get busy, Rachel."

Sarah was certainly in a tizzy. Main Street was not quite that devoid of decor, but the murals were to be a lovely extra touch. "Well, let's think. There has to be a simple solution. Other people can paint. Doesn't James create patterns to work from?"

"Like stencils? Yes, I believe he does."

"There you go, then. Someone can use his stencils to paint decor on each shop window."

"You, my girl, are brilliant." Sarah smacked her lips in satisfaction. "I told Chief, if anyone will pick up the torch and run for this celebration, Rachel will. Thank you so much. I'll get the stencils and other supplies over to you before you go home."

As if the decision was made and agreed upon, the formidable redhead marched to the exit.

Rachel blinked a few times before regaining her senses. "Wait, no. Mrs. Ambruster. Sarah."

Mrs. Ambruster spun back and pointed. "I realize the job is too much for one person, but you are crafty and talented. And most of all, dependable. Dependable Rachel. That's what I said to Chief. I'll call a few people to help you. What about that nice vet? Jake Colter. Civic duty is good for his business. Yes, yes. Great idea."

"Jake?" Before Rachel could release another protest, Sarah Ambruster blew out of the office like a tornado, leaving destruction in her path.

Rachel's path anyway.

Jake was right. They had been thrown together way too many times for this to be a coincidence.

What was going on? Who was responsible?

And why did she get a fluttery feeling in her stomach at the thought of spending more time with Jake?

During their impromptu spaghetti dinner, when Jake was his humorous self and Daley was simply adorable, Rachel had begun to think they could, at least, be cordial. Jake had even jokingly reminded her to lock her doors. Rachel hadn't. Just in case Daley walked in her sleep again, she wanted the child to have a safe place to land.

Moose, the affable retriever, had appeared at her door twice since that night. She'd returned the dog to Jake, though she hadn't stayed to play, regardless of Daley's pleadings. Even though some part of her wanted to linger, she couldn't. After a brief greeting and a laugh about the dog, she'd left for other appointments.

It was best not to stir up the past.

Yet someone in this town was trying to.

Later that evening, when Rachel arrived home with the stencils and paint supplies in the back of her Hyundai, she was still trying to work this one additional task into her overloaded schedule. Yes, she could paint, and even draw if necessary, but time was not on her side. Easter, though, was massively important to this town and she would get the job done. Even if she was painting windows all alone with a flashlight at two in the morning.

As she stepped out of her car, she registered no surprise at all to be greeted by a big, shaggy red dog. Moose.

Rachel couldn't help but smile and took a moment to rub the shiny, soft ears. The massage seemed to send Moose into a complete relaxation state. With an *oof*, he slithered to the grass, eyes closed.

"No, my friend. Get up. You're going home." Maybe she should buy some doggy treats to keep on hand.

Irritated at being hornswoggled by Mrs. Ambruster, she'd have to talk to Jake anyway. Walking the dog home was as good an excuse as any. They'd practically worn a path already.

Interestingly, the trip got easier each time.

When she and Moose stood at the back door, wondering if Jake was home yet, she again noticed the messy patio. An old broom leaned against one corner behind a faded lawn chair. Taking the broom, she swept down the cobwebs and pushed the leaves into a pile.

The door scraped open. "You're hired."

She glanced up to see Jake smiling at her, still in his scrubs. As if an ocean didn't divide them, she returned the smile.

"The dog again?" he asked.

Moose flopped at his feet, ears drooping, as if he knew he was in trouble.

"Yes." Rachel leaned the broom against the wall. "How does he get out?"

"I don't know. His name should be Houdini, like his little owner who has already figured out how to bypass the child-safety locks I put in."

Rachel gasped. "Has she walked in her sleep anymore?"

He gave a beleaguered shake of his head. His dark hair needed a cut. "Only in the house. I caught her a couple of nights ago before she got out the door."

Alarmed, Rachel said, "That's scary, Jake."

"Tell me about it. I also suspect she's the one letting Moose out."

He stepped aside and motioned for her to enter. Without argument this time, she did. They had things to talk about, aware that most of the awkwardness of before had disappeared.

"I called her pediatrician in Tulsa. He didn't seem too worried, thought the sleepwalking was probably exacerbated by the move. He said if she didn't stop soon to bring her in for a consult."

"I hope he's right. How do you sleep, knowing she might take off like that?"

"Lightly. With one eye and both ears open."

No wonder he looked tired all the time.

Regardless of his fatigue, that short, scruffy beard looked handsome, manly.

"Give me a couple of minutes to get out of these scrubs." He gestured toward his shirt, which was spotted with something she wouldn't question. "There's iced tea in the fridge." Then, with a pensiveness that gave her pause, he said, "Don't leave, okay?"

"I won't. We need to talk."

His feet made pounding noises as he raced up the stairs.

Rachel went to the refrigerator for the tea but noticed moving boxes still unpacked. Unbelievable. Jake had no time to unpack, much less paint murals or work on Easter committees. What was he thinking to take on such a load? Doc was asking too much of him.

Without giving the action much thought, she opened the boxes and began to take things out. Apparently, he'd done his own packing before the move. Although he'd wrapped the breakables, everything was jumbled together.

Footsteps, much lighter than Jake's, sounded on the stairs.

"Miss Wady. Guess what? I petted two kitties today. Daddy wet me. They're soft. I want one." Her lower lip poked out as she joined Rachel. "Daddy says no."

"Sometimes daddies have to say no even if they don't want to."

"They do?" Innocent brown eyes blinked at her.

"Uh-huh. They do."

"Oh." As if she'd flipped a switch, the child noticed the box Rachel had opened and asked, "Is that a present?"

"No, baby, these are the things you brought from your other house. Guess what I found, though?" Rachel widened her eyes and feigned excitement.

"A kitty?"

Rachel laughed and pulled out a set of purple-and-pink butterfly sheets. "Are these your daddy's?"

Both small hands to her mouth, Daley giggled, eyes sparkling. "No."

Acting silly to entertain the child, Rachel held the bedding toward the dog. "Moose's?"

Daley's giggle grew to a belly laugh. "No!"

"Then, whose are they?"

"Mine." The child reached for the sheets and hugged them to herself, her delightful giggles warming a cold place inside Rachel.

There was nothing, she thought, as beautiful as a child's uninhibited laughter.

How she'd longed to hear that sound in her own home.

Jake was a blessed man, and she was glad for him. Truly happy. Even as her own heart ached.

Jake stood at the top of the stairs and listened to the conversation from below, his chest swelling with emotion. His daughter needed the influence of a woman in her life. Rachel had always, always longed for children. During their marriage, her entire focus had been on making a beautiful home and filling the rooms with kids. It saddened him that she'd never remarried and had those children. He was sadder still that he had been unable to give her the one thing she wanted most.

But at this moment, he put aside the regrets and enjoyed the gift of listening to his daughter giggle and Rachel's gentle teasing.

He'd had a long day after Doc asked him to help with a backlog of surgeries. Though he'd intended to spend the afternoon *finally* unpacking the rest of his belongings and organizing his home, he couldn't say no to his boss. Doc had cut him plenty of slack already by letting him work only mornings most days, and at full pay, with Daley on the premises. When he'd tried to thank the man, Doc claimed Jake taking his place on Easter events freed him up to handle the vet practice. Understanding now how time-consuming these town events could be, Jake saw Doc's point. With his wife's poor health and an ever-growing veterinarian practice, the man was snowed under. So was Jake.

Having been called a workaholic by both former wives, he couldn't deny that he liked staying busy. Now that he was Daley's sole parent, however, he faced a constant juggling act between work and parenting.

His daughter was his everything.

Slowly, still listening to the conversation below, Jake eased down the steps, his hair damp from the world's fastest shower.

Rachel sat on the couch, sorting linens onto his coffee table. Daley helped, as three-year-olds do, by pulling items from boxes while she chattered to Rachel.

Rachel's responses touched him. Tender, kind. Motherly.

Again, regret pinched him. Rubbing a hand down his clean shirtfront, he rounded the stairs into the living room.

"What are you girls up to?"

Both looked up and smiled. Jake's gaze fell on Rachel. His breath quickened. His pulse jumped.

What was that about?

"Sorry," she said, not looking a bit sorry. "I couldn't resist."

"I know how you are. Everything in its place."

The memory flickered between them. She tilted her head, expression pensive. He felt the pull of the past as strong as her presence in his home. Rachel. On his couch. Looking comfortable and at home. Like before.

To hurry past the confounding thoughts, he asked, "Did you, by any chance, find the dishes?"

"Two so far." She reached under the coffee table and showed him a pair of white dinner plates.

"I finded my sheets, Daddy." Daley proudly extended her favorite butterfly sheets. She'd had them nestled on her lap. Moose sat at their feet, watching with adoration, as if digging in boxes fascinated him.

"You have more sheets somewhere," he told his daughter, not wanting Rachel to think he didn't have enough sense to own more than one set of toddler sheets.

"Here." Rachel patted a neatly folded stack. "A pink set and a set of mermaids. Is that all of them?"

He nodded. "How do you fold those fitted sheets like that? I just wad them up."

She laughed. "I noticed. But if you really want to know, I'll teach you."

He rolled his eyes and gave a half grin. Properly folded sheets was not high on his list. A man had to have priorities. "Maybe another time. Right now, I need a sandwich." He saw her doubtful look and said, "Yes, I went to the grocery store and added to what I call bachelor staples. Cold cuts, peanut butter and jelly. Hamburger and hot dog stuff. Cereal. Fruit. You know. Basics." He went into the kitchen. "Want a sandwich?"

Rachel shook her head but Daley piped up, "I do, Daddy. Peanut butter."

He pointed at her. "Sounds good to me too. With trees. Rachel says you must have something green. So does dear old Dad."

"And we get wanch."

"Ranch dressing, I presume," Rachel said. "But trees?"

"Broccoli." Above Daley's head, he made a face.

Rachel pressed her lips together and went back to sorting through the boxes. "I hope you didn't mind my doing this."

"I don't. At all. You're saving my sanity."

Wondering why Rachel lingered, but not complaining, Jake made the sandwiches, poured two glasses of milk and hoisted his daughter up to the table. Moose ambled hopefully into the kitchen and collapsed with an *oof* beneath Daley's chair.

"Are you sure I can't interest you in the finest cuisine known to the human palate?" He displayed the peanut butter jar.

"Positive. But thanks. I can't stay. Not with this most recent project Mrs. Ambruster dropped on me today."

Jake swallowed a lump of peanut butter. "Don't tell me. Stenciling Easter scenes on store windows."

"She called you."

Jake's cheeks puffed as he blew out a sigh. "She called Doc. He twisted my arm."

"I figured as much. You were right, I think."

"About?"

"When you noticed one coincidence too many. Someone appears determined to push us together. I'm sorry, Jake." Her nostrils flared. "I can't imagine why they'd play matchmaker with a couple who divorced long ago."

Jake bit into his sandwich and chewed, thoughtful. The thick nutty-sweet taste soured when he thought of how he'd failed her and how deep a wound she obviously still carried. So much so that she loathed the idea of spending extra time with him.

Except she was here, unpacking for him, playing with his daughter.

The woman confused him to pieces.

After a drink of milk and a wipe of Daley's face, he said, "Scripture says to be at peace with everyone as much as it depends on us. We can be friends, Rachel. Can't we?"

Rachel heard the wistfulness in Jake's voice. For so long, she'd tried not to think about him or their marriage. Tried and failed. Now here he was in her life again and she could think of little else.

Part of her wanted to push him away again, but all the pushing away of the past had not assuaged her heartache. The more she tried to forget, the more she remembered. And grieved.

For some reason, God had brought Jake back to Rosemary Ridge. She didn't believe in cosmic coincidences any more than Jake did. God had a plan and purpose in everything. He was Sovereign, in charge of her life and Jake's.

Hadn't she learned the song "He's Got the Whole World in His Hands" in Bible school?

But since the losses, she'd struggled in her faith, although she put on a smile and kept going to church, kept praying to understand why awful things happen to good people.

Somehow, she thought if she worked hard enough, did enough to please others and the Lord, the heaviness in her soul would go away.

Deep inside, in the secret places she hid from everyone else, even God, she questioned His plans. The Bible said He gave good and perfect gifts to those who loved Him. That He worked out all things for our ultimate good.

How then could His plan include the loss of children? How could He give something so precious, perfect, and good and then snatch it away?

Even now, she was as bewildered as ever. Yet, she yearned to be close to Jesus, was profoundly grateful for His sacrifice and resurrection that Easter represented, and knew she needed Him more than her next breath. He *was* her next breath. He held her life, all life, in the palm of His nail-scarred hand.

But, was His plan *for her*, ultimately, good?

It didn't feel that way.

Oh Jesus, what do You want me to do about Jake?

"Rachel?" Jake's voice pulled her to him. "Where did you go? Am I that boring?"

"I was thinking."

"About us?" When she winced, he put his sandwich on the island. "Being friends, I mean."

"Yes." Among other, weightier topics.

Expression hopeful, his mouth twisted in a lopsided grin. "The suspense is killing me. Either that, or the huge lump of peanut butter I swallowed. You may have to call 9-1-1." He gave his chest two fist whacks. "Or do CPR. I'm open to that."

Her lips twitched. She'd forgotten how self-deprecating and funny he could be. "Let's try for good neighbors."

She couldn't want more. No matter how charming he was.

Jake's eyes held hers. His head bobbed.

"All right. Okay. That'll work. For now." He scratched at the side of his jaw. "So, when do we start painting?"

Chapter Ten

Four high school students showed up outside the Drug Store Café at seven o'clock that night to paint. Although Rachel had reservations about using teenagers, Jake seemed convinced they'd do a good job. These teens were the group also helping with his portion of the Easter egg hunt, and he was confident they wouldn't go berserk and paint dragons or rock stars on the businesses.

Sure enough, Ross, Bennie, Malea and Whitney livened up the painting party with their jostling and joking, but they stayed on task.

Across the street, where he could keep a good eye on them without appearing to do so, he and Rachel worked together on the giant windows of the furniture store.

Yes. He'd pulled a pretty slick maneuver to paint right next to Rachel. The best part? She hadn't objected. Maybe because the kids were there, listening, when he'd assigned teams as if he was the captain.

From somewhere, Rachel had commandeered portable halogen lamps to add to the illumination of streetlights. Downtown businesses were dark. Except for the fast-food place and a convenience store on the edge of town, Rosemary Ridge closed up tight by seven.

Jake glanced at his paint partner. With a narrow brush and black paint, Rachel precisely stenciled an Easter basket filled with egg shapes onto the window next to a giant bunny and "Happy Easter."

She cast a look across the street where the teens outlined Easter lily stencils and the words He is Risen.

Jake was gratified to learn that some of the business people requested religious symbols along with symbols of spring, bunnies and eggs.

"They're doing a good job," she said.

"Yep."

With a suspicious squint, she asked, "What did you promise them?"

Apparently, she'd caught his smug expression.

"Remember what Sheila said? Teens love a challenge." He carefully crossed the *T* on *Easter*. "Bribery and threats work every time."

"I figured as much. What kind of threats? Hopefully, nothing that will get us into trouble."

She hadn't asked about the bribes.

"Gentle threats." Jake let a sneaky grin slide up his cheeks.

"Such as?" She removed the large stencil and stepped back to study the resulting outline.

"The kind that said I'd beat them in a game of Horse and post their losses on social media. Kids will do anything to look good on social media."

"And they fell for it?"

That and the twenty bucks he'd offered if they painted *and* beat him at Horse.

"Hook, line and sinker. They think they can beat me. If they do, I'm toast."

Paintbrush aloft, Rachel chuckled. "What's the penalty?"

"Bragging rights, and they'll post *my* losses on social

media with really ugly pictures and obnoxious memes. Even the girls think they can take an old man like me."

They probably could. He hadn't played in a while. Too busy.

She grinned. "They can. Whitney and Malea are both athletes."

"I was afraid of that." He pulled a comical face and went back to carefully tracing letters. "They did gloat a bit when I presented the challenge."

Rachel laughed. He loved the sound, loved that she'd relaxed enough to be friendly again.

"How much do you think we'll get done tonight?"

"This block and maybe the next." Rachel gestured toward the bank on the corner. "Kids have school. We have work. We can't stay too late."

"Yeah." Daley was already yawning from her spot on the tarp he'd brought for her. She'd been upset not to paint on the windows, so Rachel had given her a watercolor brush and a notepad.

Jake hadn't asked, but he suspected Rachel had thought of his daughter beforehand and brought the washable art supplies specifically for her. They were using tempera, not watercolor on the windows.

The idea warmed him from the inside out. Rachel was such a good person. Caring, thoughtful. If only they could…

Jake slammed the lid on the next thought and did a slow spin, silently counting the blocks on Main Street and another handful of businesses on the intersecting Broadway at the stoplight.

"This could take a while," he said. "Easter isn't that far away."

"I'm hoping if we get the outlines up in the next few nights, the merchants will fill them in. I'll make the phone

calls tomorrow and ask. That way we'll have the town decorated by the weekend."

"Brilliant." Except finishing the job meant less time
for him and Rachel to be together. Was that her intent? To
escape him as soon as possible?

Crouching, he dipped his paintbrush into the container
of sky blue. "Trying to get away from me?"

Rachel paused, holding a stencil to the window with
one hand as she turned to look at him.

"Actually, no. This is fun. I dreaded adding any more
chores to my list, but tonight has been surprisingly relax-
ing and enjoyable."

"Why surprising?"

A beat passed. She turned back to the window and her art.
With a soft, throbbing voice, she murmured, "You know."

Yes, he knew. And from the way she didn't look at him
again, the subject of *them* was off-limits.

For the next three nights, Rachel met Jake and his jolly
crew of four downtown. On the fourth evening, she rushed
home from work, grabbed an apple to munch and changed
into yoga pants and a long shirt already spattered with
paint in the cheerful colors of spring.

She hurried out to her car, and as she pressed the key
fob to unlock, Rachel's gaze fell to the back wheel. The tire
was flat.

"Oh no." Her shoulders slumped.

Had she driven home on a flat? With a frown, she hoped
the tire wasn't ruined. The expense of a new one was not
in this month's budget.

Texting Jake first, she explained the problem and asked
him to start the team stenciling without her. They were
nearly finished with downtown. They couldn't stop now
for something as mundane as a flat tire.

Then she tapped in her parents' number, hoping Dad was home. As a cross-country truck driver, she never knew for sure where he was.

Mom answered. When Rachel explained the problem, hoping Dad was around, her Mom said, "Don't worry, honey. We'll take care of it."

Abruptly, her usually chatty mother hung up. She must have guests or a club meeting in progress. Mom hosted all kinds of clubs and a senior Bible-study group in her home. Like Rachel, she preferred to stay busy, especially when Dad was on the road.

Refusing to fret over the tire, Rachel perched on her front step, answering emails and posting Easter announcements on the town's website.

The spring air was crisp and clear. Red tulips, golden daffodils and bright yellow forsythia blossomed up and down the quiet neighborhood. Across the street, Mrs. Thacker's lilacs perfumed the air. The earth had awakened once more.

Beautiful spring. Thank You, Lord.

She almost wished Moose would wander over. She hadn't seen the pretty boy all week, not since the evening she and Jake had agreed to paint murals together. Was Jake locking him in the house or garage to stop his roaming? Poor dog. He so loved to explore, especially her front porch. She'd even started leaving a dish of water out in case he got thirsty.

As she added a dancing Easter rabbit GIF to the Facebook page beneath Sarah Ambruster's list of holiday activities, a pickup truck roared around the corner and came to an abrupt halt in front of her townhouse.

Rachel's heart jumped.

Daley, with Moose looking affably on, waved from her window. Every time they met, the adorable little girl greeted Rachel with the same excitement.

She had fallen hard for the bright bit of sunshine in a tod-dler's body. The dog, too, which was silly, but she was glad to see he was with his people tonight instead of trapped inside alone. That animal loved his people. And her, for some reason.

As she returned Daley's jaunty wave, she wondered if a daughter between her and Jake would have this same sunny, loving disposition.

Jake, in old paint-and-who-knew-what-stained scrubs, hopped out of the driver's seat.

"Get in," he said without preliminary. "I'll drive you. After we finish painting tonight, I'll change your tire."

Puzzled, she stood and dusted the back of her yoga pants. "My dad is coming to change it."

"Your dad's in Tallahassee."

Rachel's mouth dropped in surprise. "But Mom—"

"—called me. Said you were stranded and needed help because your dad is away."

That was odd. "I could have phoned Keaton at the tire place."

"He's closed. So's the mechanic shop. You won't get a tire repaired or changed by either of them tonight."

"Oh. Well. Okay." Grabbing her purse and keys from the disabled car, she followed Jake to his truck. When she got there, he'd already opened the passenger door.

A hand to her elbow, he helped her step up into the high cab. Familiarity quivered through her. During their dating years and marriage, Jake had insisted on being the gentle-man.

"A godly wife," he'd say when she told him the courtesy wasn't necessary, "is a gift from God. Her price is far above rubies. That's you, so I like opening your door."

She doubted if he'd felt that way in the end.

She was a Christian woman, but had she always been a godly wife?

The thought pricked her conscience. She pushed it away. "Thanks."

Without answering, Jake loped around the truck's huge front end and hopped into the driver's seat.

Rachel turned to greet Daley and Moose. Daley wiggled in her car seat and rattled with three-year-old animation about the new day care Daddy had visited.

"I wike Miss Angela. She's nice. She gots toys and kids."

"That sounds fun." Jake had told her about this afternoon's visit to a highly recommended woman who kept a few children in her home. Angela Baker was a good fit for the busy vet, although Rachel's heart pinched at the idea of Daley being cared for by a stranger instead of someone like her who loved the child.

Someone like her.

Had she lost her senses to fall for Jake's child? Wasn't she opening herself up to another broken heart? What if he decided to block her out of his life the way she'd tried to block him? What if he and Daley moved away again?

Worse, what if something terrible happened to the child? She couldn't bear to lose another.

Except Daley was not her child to lose.

When they were on the road, Jake, completely unaware of her inner struggle, declared, "It's your mother."

Still troubled, Rachel blinked a few times to reorient. "My mother? What about her?"

Jake glanced in her direction. "Don't you see? She's the one pushing us together."

"Oh, I don't think so, Jake."

Not Mom. Rachel's own mother would never do anything to cause her grief. She knew how desperately the loss of the baby and then Jake had shattered Rachel. No one knew as well as Mom.

"Think about it, Rachel. All the times we've *coinci-*

dentally shown up to the same events. Your mother knew where you would be, and she knows every person in Rosemary Ridge. With a few phone calls and a well-placed word, she could maneuver me and you into position to *accidentally* end up together."

"But—but—" Rachel began to see Jake's point. Mom and Sarah Ambruster served together on numerous committees and were members of the same clubs. "Oh."

"Are you seeing my point now?"

"Well, she and Sarah Ambruster talk nearly every day, and Doc's wife is Mom's best friend. Has been since high school."

"There you go. Doc's wife gives him a little push, your mom talks to Mrs. Ambruster, and here we are." His fingers lifted from the steering wheel and fell again.

"I can't believe Mom would do such a thing."

"Ouch." The word might have sounded humorous, but the distress in his glance was real.

"I didn't mean it that way." She didn't want to wound Jake. In fact, she constantly battled her emotions concerning him and his little girl.

The hours they spent together decorating the town for Easter, talking, joking, had begun to polish away the rough edges of resentment. Most of the time, she didn't know how she felt about Jake. She had, however, looked forward to each night this week when the pair of them exchanged conversation and turned Rosemary Ridge into an Easter-loving town.

And the time with Daley—Oh my. That child melted her. What was she going to do about Daley?

When Jake remained silent, she had to say something. "Thank you for rescuing me."

Hadn't he always, though? During their seven years together, how many times had she called on her husband and he'd come through?

Except at the end.

Jake pulled the truck into the curb outside Beverly's Boutique.

With her mind and emotions reeling, Rachel forced herself to focus on tonight's project—the massive windows displaying dressy clothes, hats and shoes for the upcoming holiday.

Beverly, bless her, had placed a galvanized bucket of pastel flowers on either side of the entry and hung a farmhouse-style Easter lily and wooden-cross wreath on the door.

In the last three days, other merchants had done similar things. From bright sunflower wreaths to a repurposed, white rocking chair holding a plastic bunny rabbit in a nest of colorful plastic eggs. At the antique store, an old-timey milk can sprouted shoots of green leaves and sprigs of vivid yellow forsythia.

Rosemary Ridge was waking to spring and looking forward to Easter.

"My pleasure." Jake pointed at her, winked, then hopped out of the truck and hurried to open her door before she could.

As he offered his arm to help her exit the high cab, his serious brown eyes captured hers. "Honestly," he said, "my pleasure."

Flummoxed, neck overly warm, and pulse reacting oddly, Rachel tore her gaze from his.

As if he hadn't rocked her world with one look and a kind touch, Jake opened the back door and lifted his daughter from her car seat.

She didn't know what Mom was up to, but she better not have some misguided matchmaking scheme in the works. Rachel and Jake could partner together on the Easter committees. They could be good neighbors. Maybe even friends. He was a nice guy and she liked him. But anything more hurt too much to contemplate.

Chapter Eleven

Jake would remember the screams for the rest of his life.

Screams that were his fault.

After finishing the downtown project, he'd driven Rachel home and gotten out to change her flat tire.

The other truck occupants tumbled out too. Daley and Moose played under the porch light on Rachel's postage-stamp front lawn. Rachel crouched next to him to assist, joking that she could have changed the tire herself. Somehow. Except she couldn't lift the wheel part. Or figure out that jack thingy. But she could do the job if she had to. After all, she owned a smartphone and smartphones have YouTube tutorials.

He'd snorted, tickled by her humor. "Why should you do the heavy lifting when you have me?"

As soon as the words fell from his lips, he hoped she hadn't taken them wrong.

She hadn't. Instead, she joked, "You have to be good for something."

"That's what neighbors are for."

"And friends," she said, drawing his attention to her.

In the shadowy light, he couldn't read her expression, but her tone was warm. If a flat tire had brought about the change, a lesser man would strongly consider puncturing the rest of them. One at a time over several days. Not that he would, but he was pleased that she finally considered him a friend.

"Hand me that lug nut, will you?" Avoiding the black tar on his hands, he scratched his chin with his shoulder and eyed the shiny bit of metal.

Rachel did as he asked. Their fingers touched. Electricity charged between them.

Her gaze flew to his. Her pretty mouth opened in a gasp.

Mesmerized, he couldn't turn away. Neither did she.

Rachel. His first love.

Good feelings had flowed around them all week. Friendship, camaraderie, whatever she wanted to call this new relationship. They'd enjoyed being together. Again.

What would happen if he leaned in and gently placed his lips on hers? Only for a second, a whisper kiss to test the waters.

In that split second of distraction, disaster struck.

The high-pitched scream of his baby girl ripped the night.

Adrenaline shot through his body. Jake leaped to his feet. Bolts and tools scattered, clanging against each other in the short grass.

"Daley!" He spun, seeking his child. Not finding her.

She was no longer in Rachel's yard.

His gut tightened. Fear exploded like fire through his veins.

"Daley, where are you?"

Half a block down, tires squealed. An engine roared. Vehicle lights disappeared around the corner.

No, no. Oh no.

"Jake." Rachel, too, had jumped up. "There. The street. Oh no." Terror raised her voice. "She's in the street."

"Dear God. Please help." He bolted for the roadway. In

the shadowy darkness, Daley's white T-shirt glowed against the pavement.

Praying, heart thudding with terror, he rushed to the child sprawled against the curb.

"Daley. Baby." The night was dark. Though streetlights helped, they cast long, deep shadows. His vision was obscured.

Jake fell to his knees. He touched her.

"Daddy. Daddy!" Sobs tore from her throat. Scrambling to get up, she reached for him.

Thank You, Lord. She was conscious and moving.

Fearful of adding to her injury, he resisted the overwhelming urge to yank her into his arms. Examine first. Comfort second.

His hands, experienced with animals, roved over her small form. "Where are you hurt? What happened, baby?"

"Moosey," she sobbed, trembling so hard that Jake thought he might lose his professional calm. "He pusheded me down."

"Moose hurt you?" Not Moose. The sweet-natured, gentle dog adored Daley. "Where?"

"My kneebow." She offered her elbow and then let out a terrible wail. "Moosey! Moosey! I want Moosey."

As he clasped his child to his chest, aware she wasn't badly hurt but trying to comprehend what had occurred, Rachel touched his shoulder. Her fingers shook. "Jake."

"What?" He looked up at her face, pale beneath the corner streetlight.

"Moose." She motioned toward the center of the street. A dark form lay curled on its side, very still. "He's hurt."

Before he could rise, Rachel pulled Daley into her arms. His child clung to his ex-wife, her head snuggled against Rachel's shoulder as she sniffed and sobbed.

"I've got her, Jake. See about the dog."

He did.

Kneeling in the dark street, he could visualize little except the fear and pain in Moose's golden eyes.

"Oh, buddy." Gingerly, he ran his fingers along the dog's body. Moose whimpered but didn't growl or attempt to move.

"I need to get you to light, buddy. Hang in there." Carefully, he slid his hands beneath the animal and lifted him against his paint-covered scrubs. Moose moaned softly. Warm, sticky liquid Jake knew to be blood oozed onto his shirt.

As gently as he could, he carried the dog to the porch light. Rachel was there, door open. "Bring him inside."

"He's bleeding. Your carpet."

"Will clean. Come in." He heard the tears in her voice. Tears he feared echoed in his own eyes.

"Daley. Where is she?" He stepped inside. His daughter leaned against the cushions of Rachel's couch, a wet paper towel against her elbow. A glass of juice sat on the coffee table in front of her.

Rachel had taken care of her.

"Her arm is scratched, but I don't see anything else. She keeps asking for Moosey."

Briefly, he closed his eyes in gratitude and relief that his little girl was not badly injured. "Thank You, Jesus."

"Yes." Rachel stroked a loving hand on Daley's disheveled hair. "Thank You, Lord, for protecting Daley. Please help Moose."

Jake seconded the prayer. Many times as a vet he'd quietly prayed over a sick or wounded animal. He considered his occupation a calling to care for God's creation.

"Where should I lay him?" He tilted his head toward Moose. The dog had begun to shiver. Beneath Jake's fingertips, he discerned a pulse, but the beat was rapid, thready, weak.

"I'll put some towels on the island. Lay him there."

She rushed up the stairs, returning in seconds with a pile of towels. She quickly spread them on the white quartz countertop.

"My house-call bag is in the truck."

"I'll get it."

He looked toward his daughter, fearful of leaving her for a second but drawn by the emergency situation with her beloved pet.

Rachel touched his shoulder again. "She's okay, Jake. Really. I'll be right back."

As tenderly as he knew how, Jake slid the dog from his arms to the towels. His hands were covered in blood. Gently, he rolled the animal to one side to assess the damage. Moose's leg was mangled. Blood oozed from beneath his leg fur. Jake had no idea what else he might find.

His child was safe, but sweet Moose was badly injured.

Remorse swamped Jake. For only a couple of minutes, he had been distracted and a disaster had occurred. His child could have been killed.

He should have been more focused on his responsibilities instead of Rachel. Instead of wishing, hoping for a change in their relationship. Instead of trying to repair the lingering brokenness between them.

Now his daughter was scared and hurting, and his dog might die.

He hadn't been able to fix Rachel before. They hadn't even been able to talk about their loss. Still couldn't. What made him think he could fix things now?

Rachel was sure her heart was breaking as she reentered her house to the sound of Daley's sobs for "Moosey" and observed Jake frantically working over the dog.

After their marriage, he'd given up his dream of veterinarian college and taken a job locally to support her and the family they wanted to have right away. When the children hadn't come in the first few years, she'd urged him to go back to school. He hadn't, believing God would soon give them the desires of their hearts.

When she'd finally gotten pregnant, they'd both rejoiced and basked in the goodness of a loving God as they eagerly prepared for their baby. They'd made wonderful plans for little Samuel as soon as they knew his gender, including his name which meant "God has heard." They'd made lists of the characteristics they planned to instill in him: godliness, integrity, wisdom, kindness and more.

He was to be their first shining accomplishment.

Instead, his too-short life had become the disappointment she could not let go of.

Jake had never complained about working at the local bank. He'd done well there and been promoted twice. But now she could see that animal medicine was his passion, his gift, his calling.

Using the rudimentary supplies in his go-bag, he worked diligently to stop the flow of Moose's blood and to stabilize the broken leg.

"Is there any way I can help you?" Leaving Daley, whose sobs had subsided to occasional sniffs, Rachel stepped up next to Jake.

Forehead glistening with sweat, he cast a worried glance toward Daley and then said, "He needs X-rays. We should get him to the clinic."

"I'll keep Daley here if you want to take Moose."

His look was as sharp as his words. "No. She goes with me."

"Okay." She tried to understand instead of being offended.

He'd had an awful scare. They both had. Her own adrenaline still pumped like a geyser. She could only imagine how much worse his fear would be.

Starting to back away, she stopped when he said, "Come with me. I may need your help."

Some of her hurt feelings settled. "I'll open the truck doors and come back for Daley."

She hurried out and then back inside. Daley waited for her at the door, slender arms up. Her little body still trembled from the trauma.

Rachel lifted her and held the house door open with her hip to let Jake and the too-still dog exit first.

He placed Moose in the bed of the truck and cushioned him with the towels.

"Will he be all right back there?" She worried the dog would jump out.

"He'll be more comfortable there than crowded onto a seat." Face grim, he added, "He's too injured and in shock to move around on his own."

Rachel's stomach clenched. Aching with concern, she buckled Daley into her car seat, patted her cheek with an assurance that everything would be okay, and climbed into the cab without Jake's hand to steady her.

At the moment, he had those gifted hands full. Courtesy was the last thing on their minds.

Jake drove safely but as fast as allowed to the animal clinic. Once inside, he rushed Moose into the X-ray room. Alerted by the radiation caution sign on the door, Rachel took Daley into Jake's office to wait.

He was gone longer than she expected.

From the kennel room, or "Colter Castle," as Jake termed his overnight-patient facilities, a dog barked and was answered by another.

Otherwise, the small clinic was eerily quiet without the hustle and bustle of daily business.

By the time Jake emerged, Daley had fallen asleep on the nap mat her dad apparently kept in his office for her.

Rachel rose and tiptoed quietly to the doorway. "Daley's asleep. How is Moose?"

Jake leaned in for a long look at his daughter. Rachel backed away. He smelled like blood.

"Calm and woozy. I started an IV and injected pain med. His leg needs surgery."

"Will he recover?"

"If all goes well and I do my job right, he should. Tonight, I'll be watching for other injuries, but right now, I'm only seeing a badly fractured leg with some deep lacerations and scrapes." He crossed to an industrial sink and began to scrub his hands. "I'll need help with the surgery. Are you up to assist? Or should I call Doc?"

"I'm here. I'm not leaving, so if you think I can do what you need, I'm willing."

"No doubt in my mind." He motioned toward Daley. "She'll be okay here, but leave the office door open. We can see her from the OR."

"Should I wash my hands or something?"

"Bathroom is on the right if you need that first. Scrub for three minutes with the available soap. I'll have gloves and a gown ready when you finish."

With a nod, Rachel headed toward the restroom.

Ten minutes later, she stood next to Jake inside the small operating room, both of them covered from head to toe in sterile paper and wearing latex gloves.

"We don't always gown up, but I take no chances with a bone injury," he said, indicating the massive amounts of antiseptic cleanser he poured over Moose's hind leg. Rachel held a metal basin underneath to catch the liquid. "Any infection could cost him his leg. Or his life."

Rachel shivered. "Wash it again."

From behind plastic goggles, his tired eyes twinkled at her. "Yes, Dr. Rachel."

"We can't lose him, Jake. Daley would be devastated."

"So would I."

"Me too." She didn't mind admitting how much she looked forward to his dog's visits. "I think he may have saved her life, Jake. For real."

"My thoughts are along the same lines. He must have pushed her down and into the curb, away from that car I saw speed around the corner. Daley's scraped but not really injured. Yet, Moose was hit by the car in the middle of the street." He nodded. "Yeah. Something happened out there that involved Moose knocking her out of harm's way. Daley might be able to tell us later for sure, but I agree with you. Moose is a hero."

For good measure, he irrigated the leg and adjacent wounds one more time. The pungent soap and antiseptic smell permeated the room. Rachel, unused to the scents, braced against reaction, her face set in stone, nostrils instructed to breathe normally.

She knew little about medicine, other than the recovery side of physical therapy, but Jake's instructions were easy to follow. A tall metal stand, covered with what he described as a sterile drape, held shiny steel instruments. He quickly named each one for her and told her not to worry, he'd remind her if she forgot.

Gloved hands in front of her as he'd instructed, she followed his lead, handing tools, gauze pads, towels as needed. When he needed an extra hand to hold Moose's leg, she provided it.

As he worked, he explained in detail the process of repairing the leg and closing the lacerations.

As Rachel watched her ex-husband's big, gentle hands and listened to his quiet, confident words, her chest filled with pride. Not only was Dr. Jake Colter skilled and knowledgeable, he treated his patients with tenderness and care.

"Will you check on Daley?" He glanced up. "Please."

Even during the intensity of emergency surgery, his thoughts were not far from his child.

He was a good dad. A great dad.

Hadn't she known he would be?

Careful to touch nothing but the front of her gown, Rachel stepped to the doorway and peaked across the hall.

"She's still sleeping."

Without looking up from the fractured bone, he nodded. "Thanks."

They worked on, for what seemed like hours. Rachel's neck and back began to ache. She could only imagine how much more strain Jake was under.

He didn't complain, so she didn't either.

Twice her stomach grew queasy and she had to turn her head. The blood didn't bother her but the drill to insert the pin in Moose's tibia did.

Jake noticed. "You okay? I can do the rest alone if you need out."

She clenched her teeth. Swallowed the nausea. "I'm fine."

When at last he said, "We're almost finished," she breathed a heavy sigh.

He turned his head. "Tired?"

"A little."

His gaze swept her. "A lot. Take a break."

"Not till you do."

With a weary smile, he wrapped what he called a bandage cast around the pinned tibia. She knew the tibia was broken in two places, because he'd told her so, and would heal faster if pinned. Dogs were hard to keep immobile, a necessity for a broken leg. Thus, the pins for stabilization and faster healing.

"Is it all right if I start cleanup?" The room was a jumbled mess of opened packages and used supplies.

"You'll be my favorite assistant if you do."

The remark, though casual as he'd intended, caused a twitter of pleasure.

Stepping away from the metal table, Rachel gathered the disposables into a trash bag and tossed the used instruments into a silver metal basin and set them in the huge industrial sink filled with disinfectant water.

When at last they stripped away the surgical gowns covering their dirty clothes, the clock on the wall read past midnight.

Both rotated their shoulders at the same time. And laughed through their fatigue.

"Let's go home," he said.

Even though the words sounded too personal, too cozy, Rachel didn't argue.

Rachel carried the sleeping Daley to the truck while Jake settled Moose onto the back seat next to her. This time, the drugs kept him comfortable and calm. The dog was too woozy to care.

"Drive to your house," Rachel said. "I'll help you get them inside and then cut through the alley home."

"Are you sure?"

"I insist."

With a heavy sigh, he nodded. "Thanks."

The short drive home was somber. The adrenaline high was starting to subside, leaving them both exhausted.

Nothing sounded as good right now to Rachel as a hot shower and a long sleep. She hoped her mind would settle enough to let the latter happen without bad dreams.

"I'll see to your tire in the morning."

Rachel looked at Jake, his profile in relief from the dash

lights. "Forget the tire. I can get a ride to work and figure out the tire later."

"Then, I'll drive you to work."

"Okay." She was too emotionally spent to argue.

As they passed the sign leading into their neighborhood, Daley stirred and suddenly cried out. "Moosey. Moosey!"

"Shh, baby." Rachel turned in the seat. "Moosey's asleep."

Hands and feet flailing, Daley strained toward the inert dog on the seat next to her. "Moose died. The car killt him."

Another ear-splitting wail reverberated through the truck cab.

Rachel unbuckled her seatbelt and reached back to touch the child with a calming hand. "No, sugar, he's not dead. He's asleep. Daddy gave him some medicine."

"I want him. Moosey. He died. The car hurted my Moosey." Gaining momentum, near hysteria, she kicked and cried even more.

Jake pulled the truck to a hard stop in his driveway. "I'll get her."

Quickly, before Rachel could decide the best course of action to calm the child, he hopped out and jogged to his daughter's side. As he took her from the seat and started toward the house, she wailed and struggled, begging for her Moosey.

Nothing they said could convince her that the dog was alive.

Rachel's heart ached for the traumatized child. Whatever she'd seen happen had taken a toll on her little mind.

Over one shoulder, Jake asked, "Will you come in and stay with her while I take care of Moose?"

How did he manage all this by himself? "She needs you, Jake. Take her up to bed. I'll bring the dog."

"No. Leave him. If he awakens and starts to thrash, he

could reinjure himself. He's strong and heavy. I'll come back for him once Daley calms down."

He pressed the crying Daley into his shoulder and uttered shushing sounds, murmuring reassurances that Moose was okay.

Rachel followed him inside and up the stairs. This was the first time she'd entered this personal space, although the layout was the same as her townhouse.

Daley's room, on the left end of a short hallway, was a jumble of toys and boxes, her bed rumpled and loaded with stuffed animals, including the bunny she'd carried to Rachel's house that first day.

Jake had his hands full with work, volunteering, settling into a new home, and parenting this little girl.

While Jake got the child into her pajamas, Rachel found a lidded cup and filled it with water from the hall bathroom. She also located a washcloth and some band-aids.

Returning to the bedroom, she found Daley calmer. When the little girl saw the water cup, she reached for it.

Rachel sat on the edge of the low toddler bed and held it for her. "Here you go, sweetie, and you know what else I brought?"

"Moosey?" New tears welled in Daley's eyes.

"I'll get him." With a nod toward Rachel, Jake left the room, the sound of his footsteps disappearing rapidly down the stairs.

Rachel held up the box of colorful cartoon bandages. "Let's fix your elbow, okay?"

Daley sniffed. "It hurts."

"I know, baby, but a cold washcloth will feel good and make it all clean."

"And a Snoopy?"

"Yes." Rachel hoped there were Snoopy bandages in that box.

There were.

To further comfort the little girl, she snugged the stuffed rabbit, Mr. Bunny, against Daley's side. Daley wrapped an arm around the toy and burrowed down into her pillow. Tears stained the sweet round face.

While Rachel doctored the child's scrapes, she talked soothingly about Easter and made up a story about Jesus and Mr. Bunny and brave little girls.

"And Moosey." Daley's eyelids began to droop.

Rachel brushed the soft hair away from her face, over and over again. "Oh my yes, and Moosey, the bravest dog of all."

Daley's eyelids came up one more time. "Miss Wady?"

"Yes, baby?"

"I wuv you."

A lump clogged Rachel's throat. "I love you too."

What else could she say under the circumstances?

Long after Daley breathed the deep breath of sleep, Rachel continued brushing the baby-soft hair back from her tearstained cheeks, heart full of this child and longing for the children she didn't have.

Did she love this little one, even though Daley did not belong to her?

Yes, she did. The knowledge both filled her heart and set her nerves atremble.

Chapter Twelve

❧

Jake took the dog crate from the garage and toted the large wire structure up the stairs to his bedroom, the best way possible to keep an eye on the dog and watch for other injuries. If Daley was still awake and insistent on seeing Moose, he'd be close by.

Granted, Jake's sleep would be fitful and short, but if Moose had saved Daley from the car as he and Rachel believed, the pup deserved around-the-clock vet care.

Once Jake had settled the dog in the crate and made sure he was comfortable and stable, he scrubbed his hands again and headed back to his daughter.

Thank You, Lord, for Rachel. If she hadn't been with him, he wasn't sure how he would have managed.

Since Mallory's death, he'd found a way to do whatever he had to do, but Rachel had made things much easier tonight.

As he walked down the hallway toward Daley's room, all was finally quiet.

Had Rachel gotten his daughter to sleep again?

Jake paused in the doorway of Daley's room. Rachel sat on the edge of the bed, her side to him, face averted as she gazed down at Daley. As gently as a mother would do, she stroked his baby's hair and whispered something he couldn't hear. Daley's long lashes lay still against her tearstained cheeks.

His chest filled. He didn't know what got to him the most, Rachel's tenderness or the tears on his child's face.

Thank You, Jesus. Thank You, thank You, for protecting my child when I didn't. I won't let that happen again.

Yet there was the problem of Rachel.

He could not deny that he felt something for her still. Or maybe all over again.

Yes, she was pretty, but her beauty was secondary to her character. To *her*. To the way they had once fit together so perfectly.

He must have stirred or made a sound because Rachel turned her head toward him and then stood.

Softly, she said, "She's asleep."

Feeling all kinds of tender emotions he didn't know what to do with, Jake stepped in and stood next to her. Both stared down at the beautiful sleeping princess.

"She's my life," he said quietly. "My whole existence."

"I understand."

He heard the throb in her voice and knew she did understand. She would feel the same if Daley was her child. Rachel would have been a wonderful mother.

He wanted to slide his arm around her waist and let her lean into him, but resisted. Trauma had brought them closer together tonight, but they were still on shaky ground, the past between them like a wall neither knew how to scale. Jake didn't want Rachel to grow cold and distant again.

"Thank you for being here."

"I'm glad I could be." He heard her swallow, her eyes still on Daley. "She's precious, Jake. You've done an amazing job with her."

"Have I?" Struggling with the might-have-beens of tonight, he rubbed a hand over the back of his aching neck. "If I'd been on alert, this wouldn't have happened."

"You don't know that for sure," she said quietly. "Life is full of the unexpected."

"I pray a prayer of protection over her every day. If that car would have hit her—" He couldn't even go there in his head.

Rachel reached for his hand, surprising him, although he relished the comforting touch of her skin against his. "But Jake, she wasn't hit. God answered your prayer this time."

He believed God answered every prayer, although not always in the way we wanted. But saying so might stir old memories of their loss, so he only said, "Moose."

"Yes. A hero in dog disguise."

"He gets steak for the rest of his life."

She smiled a sweet smile, turned to leave, but seemed magnetized to his daughter. She bent low and kissed Daley's forehead.

Jake thought his heart would come out of his chest.

Mallory used to do the same thing. Every single night.

She'd been a loving mother. It was her husband—him— she wasn't wild about.

In a quiet rustle of paint-spattered clothes, Rachel straightened and turned to look at him, the tenderness in her gray eyes undeniable. Gold sunbursts, like lights into her compassionate soul, surrounded her dark pupils.

The urge to kiss her rose again, a foolish urge that could only cause trouble.

Neither of them wanted a repeat of the past.

Lips barely moving, though they definitely held his attention, she asked, "What happened to her mother? Did she have cancer?"

Rachel had a fear of cancer. Too many friends and family members had died of the terrible scourge, including her beloved grandmother. Rachel never missed a medical checkup and had fretted at him every year to get his.

"Not cancer." Jake motioned toward the door with his chin. Even as late as the hour was and as tired as he was, he wasn't ready to let Rachel go. He wanted to tell her about Mallory.

Back downstairs, he took two bottles of water from the fridge, set one in front of her and uncapped the other. "You hungry?"

"Maybe. What do you have?"

Squinching his eyes, he scratched his jaw. "You already know the answer to that. Peanut butter and jelly? Apples? Mac and cheese, but we'd have to cook it."

"PB and J." She slid off the stool. "I'll make them. You're exhausted."

"So are you." He refused to sit down; instead he worked alongside her and joked about his culinary expertise. He needed a few minutes to organize his thoughts before he could tell her about Mallory, about his failures as a husband and as a protector.

Though why he worried about her reaction, he didn't know. Rachel had already experienced his failures and knew them better than anyone.

When the sandwiches were prepared and glasses of milk poured, they settled across from each other at the small rectangular table.

Jake took a big bite of his sandwich and chewed while he decided how to begin.

"If the subject of Daley's mother is too painful," she said, "we'll discuss something else while we eat this delicious gourmet sandwich." With a twinkle in her eyes, she bit into the PB and J.

"She died in a plane crash."

The brick in his gut that was Mallory's death caught fire and burned. He put his sandwich down.

"A plane crash," Rachel murmured, face twisted in sympathy. "Jake, how terribly tragic. I'm sorry."

"So am I. For more reasons than one." He sucked in a breath and let the truth gush out. "Her death was my fault. I put her on that plane. If not for me, Daley would still have a mother."

A giant lump of peanut butter lodged in Rachel's throat. She reached for the milk.

After a deep, cleansing drink, Rachel grappled with Jake's disturbing statement, knowing it could not be true.

"How are you responsible for a plane crash?"

He rocked back in the chair and looked upward toward the small pendant light hanging over the table. When his gaze returned to hers, his face was sad, his voice grim.

"We'd gone on a second honeymoon of sorts. At least that's what I called the trip. Mallory called it my last-ditch chance to fix our marriage. She didn't want to go at all, but I convinced her for Daley's sake."

This was news. His second marriage had been failing.

"Was Daley with you?"

"With my parents in Lakeside." Lakeside was a larger community next to Willow Lake, thirty miles away. "I thought the trip to the Rockies would give us time to revisit the good things about our life together."

"You loved her."

"I did. Or thought I did. I wanted to. Maybe I worked too much like she claimed and wasn't home as much as I should have been. I was faithful, even though she said work was my mistress."

"I know that about you, Jake. Your faithfulness." She'd never worried about him cheating. "What about Mallory?"

He closed his eyes, his breathing heavy, his lips angled downward. His reply was a whisper, "I didn't know until—after."

"I'm sorry." She was at a loss for anything else to say.

"Me too. Learning he's not enough does something awful to a man."

Rachel's heart twisted for him. Had she made him feel the same way?

"Were you on the plane with her?"

He shook his head. "She'd gotten sick the day before. When she wasn't better the next morning, I asked a friend with a private plane to fly her home. He was going that way and could get her to the doctor in a few hours. Since he only had one spare seat and I had our car, I drove back to Tulsa. The plane went down in the New Mexico mountains. No survivors."

The awfulness of the tragedy settled like a heavy cloud over the kitchen. Outside a car motored past. The heating unit stirred to life.

Rachel's chest pinched with sympathy.

"I still don't understand how you're to blame, Jake."

"I put her on that plane. She hated flying, but I insisted she go."

"Did she object?"

"No, not much. She was really sick, but that's irrelevant. She died. I didn't."

"I don't know what to say except you're blaming yourself when you shouldn't. You aren't in control of life and death." She touched the back his hand where he gripped the tabletop. "If you had both been on that plane, Daley would be an orphan."

"My brain knows that. My heart still argues. How do I ever explain Mallory's death to Daley?"

"I don't know a lot about children, but Daley loves her daddy, and when the time comes that she asks questions, I think you'll find the right words. You cared for her mother. She was sick. You tried to do what was best for her by getting her to help as quickly as possible."

A beat passed and then two. She wanted to convince him that he wasn't to blame but could see by his expression that he believed he was.

After a brief silence, when she didn't know what else to say, Jake flipped his hand over and laced his fingers through hers. "Enough about me. Why are you still single?"

In other words, he didn't want to talk about his late wife or her death anymore.

Rachel didn't exactly want to discuss her lack of love life either. "No takers."

His laugh was short. "I don't believe that."

The subject was a sore one, but no sorer than what he'd shared with her.

"I dated a few times after—" she shrugged "—you know. But no one fit." Each date had left her emptier than before, so she'd stopped going out altogether, and instead settled into a routine of work, church and volunteering.

No other man had fit like Jake had.

With an inner shake of her head, she refused to walk that road again. She and Jake were history. That direction lay overwhelming grief and endless sorrow.

She tugged her hand from his and pushed away the mostly eaten sandwich. "I should get home. My alarm goes off in less than five hours."

As if he suspected she was avoiding an uncomfortable topic, he searched her face for one more long moment until, finally, she looked away and stood to her feet.

"Mind if I check on Daley one last time?" She could not leave until she did.

"I'll go with you."

She led the way, aware that he came up the carpeted stairs behind her, his fingers pressed gently to her back as if taking care that she didn't fall.

Ever the protector.

A protector who had put his wife on a plane to help her only to send her to a calamitous death.

Poor Jake. She knew him well enough to know he'd beat himself up over that for a long time, maybe forever.

The rumbling, tumbling yearning toward this man she'd known so well started up inside her again.

They could be friends. She would not allow herself to think of more. She couldn't. Not with the secret she'd buried since his departure.

At Daley's doorway, she was acutely aware of Jake's shoulder touching hers as they gazed at the slumbering child. The Snoopy bandage shown on Daley's elbow. Mr. Bunny's ear was in her lax mouth. She breathed slow and deep, her innocent face relaxed in sleep.

Rachel exchanged glances with Jake. A soft, loving smile played around his mouth. His heart was on his face.

Without speaking, they took the stairs down and to the back patio doors.

"I'll walk you home."

"No need. Go to bed."

"Then, I'll watch from here to be sure you get inside safely."

A part of her wanted to laugh at him. She'd been taking care of herself for twelve years. But her belly curled in pleasure at the notion that he still wanted to protect his ex-wife.

He *needed* to do this, so she'd let him.

A south breeze blew hair across her face.

Before she could shake it away, Jake looped the stray lock behind her ear. His fingertips lightly lingered on her skin.

He used to do that often. As if he relished touching her skin. Was he remembering as she was?

Her gaze lifted to his. His expression was warm, tender, reminiscent.

Yes, he remembered.

In spite of her own misgivings about *them*, tonight's emotional upheaval still pulled at her. The story concerning his latest loss played on her emotions too.

"Thank you for telling me about Mallory."

A beat passed while he watched her with that same warm brown gaze. Then, never looking away, he pushed her hair back again.

Tingles raised goosebumps on her neck and shoulder.

"Thank you for listening. For being here tonight for me, for Daley, Moose." His smile was bittersweet. "For being my friend again."

It was the *again* that got her. They'd once been such good friends.

They were standing inches apart and the sudden need to comfort him overrode her caution.

She slid her arms around his waist and hugged him. Out of kindness. Out of compassion. Friend to friend.

Jake's response was instant. His arms came around her back and pulled her close.

Though alarm bells clanged like a fire engine inside her brain, Rachel rested her head on his strong chest.

Against her ear, his heart thudded strong and solid while her pulse rattled against her collarbone like marbles in a can.

His warm breath fluttered against her hair, a contrast to the cool night breeze.

She stilled. Had he kissed her hair? She thought he had.

Instead of withdrawing as she should have, she rested there in his arms, a dozen conflicting emotions flying through her like wild birds afraid to land.

"Rachel."

Later, she'd wonder if she imagined the longing in his tone. A longing that matched her own.

Whichever, the sound was all the reminder necessary to break through the spell.

She pulled away. "I have to go."

"Yes."

But neither moved.

A tiny curve appeared on his mouth. He leaned in, touched his lips to her forehead before stepping back, smile still in place, still tender. "Good night."

It was only a kiss on her forehead. Yet, the feel of his warm mouth against her skin unleashed a torrent of longing so intense tears rose in her throat.

She managed a "Good night," then spun and hurried across his backyard and through the alley toward her townhouse, aware every moment of Jake's watchful eyes and that she was beginning to want something she could not have.

Chapter Thirteen

Early the next morning as the sun squeezed a hazy light across a horizon filled with clouds, Jake knelt next to Rachel's car, still hiked up on the jack from last night. His tools and the lug nuts lay scattered on the green grass.

Rachel's house remained dark. She must still be asleep. Either that or she pretended not to know he was out here.

Had he overstepped? Sent her back into her cold igloo to hibernate?

Last evening had been a strange one. They'd gone from cheerfully painting Easter baskets to operating on his dog and finally to a midnight kiss.

He wanted to blame the forehead kiss on exhaustion and the near disaster with Moose and Daley. Wanted to but couldn't. He'd used every bit of willpower he had to avoid kissing her lips. Though he'd buried the feelings deep for a long time, he remembered how much he'd once loved kissing Rachel.

Something, he thought, had shifted between them last night. An easing, perhaps. Warm and caring, even if not completely relaxed. They'd worked as partners in the operating room and he'd gone to sleep with the vision in his head of Rachel tenderly soothing his daughter.

She'd made him feel better about Mallory's untimely death too.

Was there any hope that they could put aside the damage of their shared past?

He wanted to. But was a true reunion of hearts possible?

The massive elephant in the room that neither of them dared approach remained a major issue. If he brought up the topic of their son, would he lose her all over again?

He positioned the spare tire onto the wheel, metal clanking against metal, his head filled with too many thoughts to process at once.

His body was tired, but his brain had already kicked into high gear, eager to get to the clinic, pick up supplies and get busy. Work was his solace, his refuge when he felt overwhelmed, though since becoming a single father, he strove for better balance. One of the main reasons he'd taken the job with Dr. Howell.

Today, however, he was overwhelmed and needed the distracting focus of his job. But before he jumped into work, he'd contact the police department and file a report about last night's incident, though without having seen the vehicle, he didn't figure it would do much good.

As he spun the final lug nut on, a voice came from behind him.

"How's Moose?"

Still squatting next to the car, he looked over his shoulder at Rachel.

His stomach dipped.

Against the barely risen sun, she was a white-robed vision, her long dark hair brushed smooth against the fluffy fabric. She appeared rested and refreshed, though she couldn't have been. Not after their late night.

She held two mugs. *Two.* One for her. One for him. Steam and the faint scent of coffee rose from them.

Pleasure bloomed in his belly.

"He's better. Awake and wanting to get up and out of that cage." After giving the nuts one final tightening with the tire tool, he rose to his feet and stepped closer.

She offered the coffee mug. "Any complications?"

Taking the warm drink in his sooty hands, he sipped. "None. He looks pretty forlorn, but when he saw Daley, his tail thumped madly."

"He loves her."

The hot brew felt good to his throat and hands. Steam rose against his ungroomed face. He needed to trim his beard but didn't have time. "She says he jumped on her when the car came too fast. He knocked her down against the curb."

Rachel's head dipped, her expression growing soft. "As we thought."

If she was mad at him about the kiss, she didn't show it.

"He's a hero, for sure. I gave him extra treats and some pain meds first thing."

"Where's Daley?"

"I dropped her at day care for a few hours while I make house calls."

An anxious frown crossed Rachel's pretty features. "Is she okay there?"

"I feel good about the place. She likes having other kids to play with. She bounced right inside Miss Angela's house and barely waved goodbye."

"Okay." Rachel took a drink from her cup. "Last night was wild. I'm glad everyone is okay or, in Moose's case, will be."

"What time do you head to work?"

"Seven thirty. But if you need to go earlier—"

"I don't," he interrupted before she could find an excuse not to ride with him.

Was he wrong to push her to settle things between them?

He needed to make peace with her. To resolve the hurt and anger that had festered between them for far too long. He hadn't understood how much their breakup still affected him—and her—until he'd seen her again. Now he needed to somehow fix the problem.

Fix. He laughed ruefully on the inside. The only thing he could fix was this flat tire.

Yet, he was compelled to try.

He handed her the coffee mug. "Thanks for that. I needed a jolt."

"What you really need is two days' sleep."

"Not happening for a while."

"Work?"

Work had been a contentious subject between them before. Between him and Mallory too.

"I've learned my lesson," he said.

She raised a disbelieving eyebrow. "No more overtime? Even though you are now a country vet who makes house calls?"

"Well, emergencies arise."

Her nostrils flared. "They always did, even when you weren't a vet."

Taking the coffee cups, Rachel turned toward the porch, her long white robe swirling above her ankles.

Had he stuck his foot in his mouth? Said the wrong thing? Was she upset?

So much for reparations.

Jake rolled the wheel to his truck and tossed the flat into the back, intending to have the hole repaired for her. An excuse to come back.

Rachel stood halfway between her car and the porch, watching him. "If you need to leave earlier," she said, "you can pick me up anytime in the next thirty minutes. I have a key to my office."

His mood lifted. All he needed to do was shower and change. And maybe grab some banana-nut muffins from the bakery. Did she still love them?

"Seven thirty's good," he said. "See you then."

During work at the physical therapy office that morning, Rachel's thoughts were never far from Jake and the events of the previous night. Even her boss, Kim, noticed her distraction. When Rachel explained about Daley's near-miss and the dog's injuries, leaving out the late night and worrisome hug-turned-forehead-kiss, Kim grinned as if she knew a secret.

"You and the new vet are getting pretty chummy, huh?"

Kim was a relative newcomer to Rosemary Ridge, so, before rumors got started, Rachel told her what no one else apparently had.

"Jake is my ex-husband, Kim. We divorced years ago. When he moved back, Doc Howell volunteered him for the Easter committee and we got stuck on the same subcommittees. End of subject."

But was it really? Hadn't there been more to last night than a divorced couple forced together by circumstance?

Kim pressed two fingers to her lips. "Oh. My big mouth. I'm sorry, Rachel."

"Not a problem." Except it was. *She* was having a serious problem with anything related to Jake Colter. And Daley. And Moose. All of which was like walking into a raging forest fire and hoping to come out unscathed. Yet, she didn't know how to stop without behaving like a bitter old woman with a cold, unforgiving nature. "Like I said, the divorce was years ago. We're cordial."

"I thought so. Everyone's talking about the two of you and how cute you are together, so I assumed—" She bounced a fist against her mouth. "Sorry. Time for Kim to shut up and go torture the next poor client."

The joke brought a smile to Rachel, but inside, she wondered. Had she and Jake become the topic of gossip?

Ridiculous.

Struggling with the odd statement and Mom's insistence on the phone this morning that she had nothing to do with any matchmaking conspiracy, Rachel used her lunch break to clear her head by strolling down Main Street to admire her team's handiwork.

Every window reminded her of Jake and Daley and the fun they'd had "painting the town," as he liked to joke.

Most likely, townspeople had noticed them working together on the windows. That's where the rumors got started.

With only a few weeks left until the latest Easter in memory, Rosemary Ridge bloomed with spring and Easter decor. Even on this cloudy, chilly day when she was glad for her denim jacket, the colorful flowers, eggs and other decorations were enough to cheer even the most troubled mood.

At Beverly's Boutique, she stopped to admire the whimsical painting of a rabbit in a blue top hat and coattails, holding a basket of colored eggs in one hand and a rainbow-striped umbrella in the other. This had been Daley's favorite of all the designs they'd done.

"Right pretty, ain't it?"

A short, wiry man in cowboy attire and a hat as big as he was stopped next to her.

Wink Myrick was one of a trio of senior citizen brothers who seemed to know everyone in the county. "Hello, Wink. Yes, I'm really pleased with the way they turned out since we had to use stencils instead of a real artist."

"You and those young ones did a fine job. That new vet

too." He winked. "God works in mysterious ways, don't He?"

Rachel blinked. What was that about?

Wink tipped his hat. "Got to be rambling. Catfish is expecting me for lunch."

The diminutive cowboy meandered on down the street in the direction of the Drug Store Café, where his youngest brother, a trained chef, dished up culinary delights and really good meatloaf, leaving Rachel to stare at the boutique window and wonder about his strange comment.

Not that she should wonder much. Everyone in town knew the three Myrick brothers were a tad eccentric.

Shaking off the encounter, she admired Beverly's clothing displays. Though the Easter painting took up a third of the window, the other side featured dress-up clothes, or "church clothes" as Mom would call them.

Beverly pushed open the door and peeked out. "Might as well come in and buy something. Easter's coming."

Rachel grinned. "Can't today, but I'm tempted."

She'd love a new Easter outfit.

"I have a lavender floral exactly your style. That dress would be gorgeous on you for Easter." She motioned toward a fancy, ruffled princess dress. "Don't you think Jake's little girl would be adorable in that pink?"

Was everyone in town pushing her toward Jake Colter?

Or was Beverly's question simply a smart businesswoman's way of encouraging a sale?

"Yes. Very pretty." Determined to end the conversation right there before paranoia set in, Rachel waved and headed back to work.

She'd taken the walk to clear her head. Instead, she was more flummoxed than ever.

After the hug last night that became more than a friendly gesture of comfort, her insides were as tangled as spaghetti.

Were other people seeing something she wasn't? Most of them knew that she and Jake had once been married. They also knew the couple had lost a second trimester baby and divorced a year later. Why would they want to intentionally force Rachel to revisit old heartaches and losses?

Later, during a lull between therapy clients, she opened the Bible she kept in her desk, searching for…something. Answers, comfort, assurance. She wasn't sure what she needed.

Jake Colter had moved back to Rosemary Ridge and messed up her carefully ordered world. Now he and their shattered history stayed in her thoughts continually. All day. Every day.

If the Lord had answers in the Bible, she wasn't finding them.

At three thirty, Keaton from the tire shop walked into the physical therapy office, Rachel's car keys dangling from his index finger.

"Tire's repaired. You picked up a nail. You're all good now and the spare's back in your cargo hold."

"What? Who? How?" But she knew.

"Jake Colter." He grinned. "Nice guy," he said and then sauntered out the door, whistling.

Heat flushed her neck. She shouldn't have been surprised but she was. Pleasantly.

How in the world had Jake had time with his busy schedule to deal with her car? She'd expected him to be too focused on his job. Yet, he'd thought of her instead.

Oh, Jake. You are messing with my head.

"Thanks," she murmured, though Keaton was long gone.

After work, she dropped off some mending for Mom that she'd carried in her car for a week and wrestled with the notion of paying a visit to the wounded dog and the traumatized child.

Not specifically to see Jake, though she needed to thank him for the repaired tire.

As a neighbor and friend should.

If her nerves jittered a little to think about seeing Jake again, she blamed the condition on their awkward situation. Although seeing Jake wasn't awkward anymore.

She could be cordial, friendly even, as long as she guarded her heart. She'd once loved him with her whole being. So much so that she never, ever wanted to hurt that way again.

Since her mother lived on the opposite side of town, Rachel had to drive back through downtown to go home. On the way, she passed the Pizza Plaza. Jake had a full day of work including farm visits. He'd told her so this morning on the ride to work.

She owed him for the tire repair. The least she could do was provide food.

Making a U-turn, she returned to the Pizza Plaza and went inside.

Jake squinted at the clock for the first time in hours. Four emergencies had come in after noon and three required surgery. He'd taken on the surgeries while Doc treated the regular appointments.

Seven thirty, far past closing time. He felt the hour in every bone in his body. The late night and long day were catching up with him.

Carrying the last surgical patient, a poodle that had eaten a stuffed animal, to a kennel, he then went back for cleanup.

Doc poked his head around the door. "I'm headed home. You got this?"

"Sure." That's what the second-in-command did.

He finished the cleanup and checked the poodle and the C-section bulldog and her pups one last time before locking up and heading to the day care for Daley. He was thankful

Angela had agreed to watch her a few extra hours tonight, though he promised not to make a habit of being so late.

He hoped he could keep that promise.

Childcare was a constant source of concern for a busy country vet who might be called out in the middle of the night.

So far, he'd had none, but this was spring and if today was any indicator, accidents increased, troubled births were the norm, and animals spent more time outdoors and into everything.

A short time later, as he drove into the neighborhood, his belly dipped. Rachel's car was parked on the street in front of his house.

He exited the truck, got Daley out and started toward the Hyundai. Rachel met him in the yard.

"Your pizza's cold."

A burst of pleasure shot through his fatigue. "You brought us pizza?"

"I shouldn't have."

Un-oh. "Are you mad at me about something?"

He really didn't need to ask. He was late. The pizza was cold.

"Why should I be? I'm not your keeper." Tone crisp, her body language was stiff.

"You are angry. I still recognize the symptoms. But I have a good reason."

"You always did."

"Maybe not then, but I do now." He'd thought his reasons then were good. He'd *needed* to work, but more as an excuse to escape than the need for money. He couldn't help Rachel grieve. She wouldn't let him. Jake now realized his absences had driven the wedge between him and Rachel deeper. "Don't be mad. I didn't know you'd be here."

"Wouldn't have mattered. You would have chosen work."

He realized then that she wasn't angry about tonight or the cold pizza. She still harbored resentment from the awful time after the miscarriage. For the extra jobs he'd taken on, the late nights working in the garage, at the bank, anything to keep from losing his mind. He'd lost a child and saved his mind, but he'd also lost Rachel.

A failure.

"Guilty as charged," he said, quietly, with the heavy remorse he felt.

Daley tilted her head up toward Rachel. "Did you brought pizza for me?"

Rachel's stiffness melted as she gazed down at his daughter. "I did." She pushed the pizza box into Jake's gut and plopped a bag of salad on top. "You and your dad can warm the pizza in the microwave."

Juggling the box in the crook of one elbow, Jake reached for her jacket sleeve. "Don't you want to see Moose?"

She hesitated. "How is he?"

"Let's go see. Come on. Please." *Don't go away mad. Don't go away at all.*

Daley took hold of Rachel's hand. "Daddy said you helped make Moosey all better. He said he likes you a lot 'cause you're nice. And pretty."

Out of the mouths of babes. He hadn't said that exact thing but close enough. Daley had her own way of relaying information.

"He said that?"

She looked from him to Daley to the house and back to him.

He shrugged. "I speak truth to my daughter. Pizza's getting cold. Er."

He knew the cold-er would bring a smile, or at least a half one.

It did.

"All right. As I said, I don't know why I got upset. I'm not your keeper."

"More's the pity. I need one." He joked, but only partly. "Today was a nightmare."

He unlocked the front door, pushed inward and waited while the two ladies entered. All the while he kept up a running commentary on his busy day, hoping to convince Rachel that he really did have an excuse for the late hour.

Daley stopped in the living room and sniffed. "Something stinks."

Jake groaned. "Forgot to take out the trash."

He stuck the pizza under his daughter's nose. "Smell this instead."

Daley giggled and drew in an exaggerated sniff. A curly ponytail bounced on either side of her head. He had practiced for months to get those things even, and he was pretty proud of how easily he wrestled his daughter's hair into place these days.

An amused smile worked in the corners of Rachel's mouth. She crossed the short distance to the back patio doors and slid them open, leaving the screen secured. Jake slid the pizza onto the counter, grabbed the trash can and carried the stink out to the dumpster.

When he returned, Rachel was setting plates on the table while Daley put a napkin by each one. The bagged salad now waited in a big plastic bowl in the center of the table.

"Sorry about the trash. I was in a rush this morning."

Rachel's dark hair brushed her jean jacket as she turned toward him. Last night, her hair had smelled like a spring rain, fresh and clean.

Yeah, he remembered. Had thought about her off and on all day.

"Thank you for having my tire fixed. What do I owe you?"

He put the pizza box in the microwave and poked several buttons. The device beeped and then began the familiar hum of heating.

"This pizza should cover it. Best pay of all. I didn't have to scrounge up dinner." He pointed up the stairs. "Moose first, though."

"That's why I'm here," Rachel said, as if reminding them that she wouldn't be in his house at all if not for the dog.

The thought hurt a little, but he understood. Some heartaches don't disappear just because you want them to.

Reaching his bedroom, Daley rushed to the dog crate and stuck her fingers through the wires. Moose licked them.

"He's not died, Daddy." Daley's delighted face glowed up at him. "He wicked me."

"I see that." Jake took Moose from the crate and crouched on the floor to examine the injured leg. He was sharply aware that Rachel went to her knees beside him. Her soft perfume filled his nose and his mind. As did the woman herself.

He ran a hand along Moose's ribcage. The dog whimpered and gazed at him with sad eyes. "Sore, pal?"

"Poor thing. He must be." Rachel's sympathetic gaze met his. "Can he come downstairs with us? Or does he need to remain immobile?"

"Pwease, Daddy. I'll take care of him."

"Being around family will be good for him." If Rachel objected to being included as "family," she said nothing. She was, yet she wasn't. "With the pins, we'll let him get up and move around anyway. The key is keeping him from overdoing."

"He's okay to walk?"

"Limited walking. The stairs are out for now."

Jake scooped the dog into his arms and went downstairs.

Later, after they'd eaten dinner, Daley sat on the floor with Moose, stroking his head while Jake and Rachel cleared the table. As he watched his ex-wife moving around in his kitchen, interacting sweetly with Daley and occasionally stopping to rub Moose's ears, Jake was struck with a sudden realization. He didn't want her to leave. Ever.

He was falling in love with Rachel all over again.

Over pizza and salad, Jake told her about the emergencies that had come to the clinic late that afternoon. In spite of believing he would never change and that work would always come first, Rachel found herself sympathizing.

She shouldn't have overreacted when he arrived late. She should have taken the pizza home, called Claire and her family and invited them over to eat.

Or waited patiently.

Instead, she'd behaved like a shrew.

Lord, will the bitterness ever lift?

Until Jake's return to Rosemary Ridge, Rachel thought she had the anger under control, and then, at times like tonight, the dragon reared its ugly head and snarled. Mostly at him.

He didn't deserve that kind of treatment. They weren't married. She had no right to know where he was or if he would be late. He'd been nothing but kind and thoughtful since his return.

She was determined to do better.

"How did Doc handle all the work alone before you came?" she asked after he mentioned the number of animals they'd treated today.

"He says he wasn't this busy until I showed up. Today

wouldn't have been as hectic, but I ran into a problem this morning and was delayed at a farm."

"What happened?" His vet stories, she found, were far more interesting than discussions of his banking position had ever been.

He told her about a calving cow that had died. The farmer blamed him for not saving the animal although the cow was too far gone by the time he arrived. The best he could do was save the calf.

"The farmer called Doc. Told him not to send a greenhorn to do a vet's business anymore."

"Ouch. What did Doc say?"

Laying his food on the plate, he patted his mouth with a napkin. "Told me not to let that kind of thing bother me. Said the farmer was a cheapskate who always waited until the situation was dire before calling a vet."

"Then, stop worrying." She pointed a forkful of salad at him. "You can't heal them all."

"I know." His grin was sheepish. "Can't blame a vet for wanting to, though."

He'd carried his fixer tendencies into his veterinarian practice. A perfectionist workaholic, he'd claimed to have tempered his passion for constant labor, but Rachel wondered if he really had.

"I have to admit your job is interesting," she admitted.

"Unlike deposits and withdrawals that are protected by privacy laws?" he asked, referencing his former occupation with a teasing lift of eyebrows.

"Well…" With an answering grin, she took another slice of pizza and caught the trail of white cheese on the tip of her finger.

"Enough vet talk." He bounced fisted hands on the edge of the table. "Are we finished with the Easter stuff?"

"Pretty much. Setup is next Friday evening and then

the big events of Holy Week on that following Saturday and Sunday."

"Are we doing that? The setup?"

"I am. If you're busy at the clinic, we can handle the rest."

"I'll be there."

Would he? Or would some dog or cow or ferret get sick and need him more than she did?

She caught the last thought and argued with herself. She didn't *need* Jake Colter. Like all the other volunteers, he did his part, but she did not *need* him.

However, she realized with a jolt, she wanted him there. That's why she'd overreacted at his lateness. She'd been disappointed.

When the disturbing truth settled heavier than pizza on her belly, Daley filled the silence.

The little girl who'd quietly stuffed herself with pizza stacked a pile of uneaten pepperoni slices on the edge of her plate. "Daddy's buyden me a baket."

"Basket," Jake corrected gently.

"When?" Daley plopped a pepperoni slice onto her dad's plate and tilted her head in a fetching manner. "A-morrow?"

Rachel's mouth twitched at the mispronunciations and the clear effort to charm her father into agreeing. Three-year-olds were fun…and insistent.

"Soon." He popped the offered pepperoni into his mouth, eyes cutting to Rachel.

"And bwue eggs. And a real bunny. With ears."

Jake's eyes twinkled. He was having a hard time not laughing at the little manipulator. So was Rachel.

"Chocolate bunny maybe."

One of Daley's shoulders hitched. "Okay. Does you wike chocolate bunnies, Miss Wady?"

For some reason, Daley had decided to stick with Miss Wady as Rachel's name.

"Love them."

"Real chocolate. The dark kind." Jake's gaze moved from his daughter back to Rachel. "Not the artificial stuff."

Warmth curled in Rachel's stomach. He remembered her preference for chocolate.

She had a sudden flash of heart-shaped boxes filled with dark chocolates. Every Valentine's Day. Even the last one. She'd cried over that saved box long after they'd parted.

Did he still have the gifts she'd given to him?

Likely not. He'd been remarried. No new wife would appreciate an ex-wife's cufflinks or engraved keychain.

"I could pick up an Easter basket for her if you're busy."

Jake's expression grew solemn. "I make time for the important things, Rachel."

"Good to know." Daley deserved as much. "While you're shopping for Easter, I saw a pretty pink dress in Beverly's Boutique window today."

"I don't wear pink," he joked. "Looks terrible on me."

Rachel rolled her eyes, letting the smile come.

"I do." Daley's eyes lit up. "I wuvs pink."

"You would look so pretty in a fancy pink Easter dress."

"Pwease, daddy. A pink dress. And a bunny."

Jake laughed. "One-track mind." To Rachel, he said, "How about Saturday afternoon? The clinic closes at noon. Want to go Easter shopping? Help a dad out?"

Her instinct was to refuse, but she overrode the urge. She wanted to go. She wanted to see Daley dolled up like a princess. And whether doing so was wise or not, she wanted to spend more time with Jake.

Chapter Fourteen

Early Saturday morning, having already seen three patients and sent them on their way, Jake was restocking the clinic's medicine cabinet when Doc also experienced a lull.

The old vet was an energetic man with a thick shock of gray hair and bright blue eyes in an intelligent, time-wrinkled face. Ever the professional, he wore a white medical jacket over scrubs, the same as Jake. His coat was still clean, a sign that this morning had been slower than normal.

Jake was happy about that, considering today was the promised shopping trip with Daley and Rachel.

"Pansy's looking better. Temperature's down. I think we've beaten the staph."

Pansy was the name Doc had given a stray cat the police had brought in with a massive infection and too many fight wounds.

"That's good." As they talked, Jake checked the expiration label on a container of antibiotics. "What will you do with her when she's well?"

"Ah, I don't know. Animal shelter, I guess, unless you'd want a gentle old cat for Daley."

Jake pulled a face. "Don't say that too loud. Daley's in the office, but she has big ears. I don't need another animal."

"Hands full with Moose, I guess?" Doc ripped open a carton of animal wormer.

Jake carefully reorganized the medicines by type. Doc could be a little haphazard with the shelving process. He joked that he'd been in that clinic so long he could find what he needed in the dark and blindfolded. Jake didn't share that luxury.

"Keeping a dog that big exercised while restrained is a challenge. He tugs on the leash, wanting to cross the alley to the neighbors."

"Any neighbor in particular? Maybe a pretty brunette?"

"Now, Doc."

"I'm only asking." Doc held up both hands. "However, you've been in a mighty fine mood all week. You didn't even gripe when old Adams called you out to work his pigs in that mudhole of his."

"Part of the job."

"So how *are* things between you and Rachel? The two of you have been seen around town quite a bit lately. Folks notice."

Jake paused, one hand on another carton. "People are gossiping about Rachel and me? Seriously?"

"In a good way. Don't get riled." Doc handed him a pack of wormer. "Son, this town thinks highly of Rachel Hamby. They want to see her happy again, the way she was when the two of you were together."

Jake put the wormer into a drawer, reminding himself to label every drawer and cabinet in the place.

"I guess we weren't that happy back then, Doc." But they had been until the miscarriage.

"Well, we all know what happened. Grief is a mighty mean taskmaster. But the Lord can heal anything."

Jake rubbed a hand over the back of his neck. "I believe that, Doc. God brought me out of a real dark place after the miscarriage and divorce. Oh, the ache is still there, the questions. I can't deny that."

"How long's it been?"

Jake knew what he meant. "Twelve years, three months and fifteen days."

Doc gave him a long, sympathetic look to let Jake know the older man understood that healing didn't mean forgetting.

"You've moved forward."

"I have. But I don't know if Rachel has."

"In her own way, I figure she has. I guess you know her mama and Helen are fast friends. Sue Ann tells us things."

"About Rachel?"

Doc nodded, the box of medicines apparently forgotten for the moment. "Did you know she makes cards and gifts for the nursing home and sews blankets for preemies over in Centerville Hospital?"

He knew about the nursing home. She'd always had a heart for the elders, as she termed senior citizens. She'd looked after her grandparents until they passed. "Didn't know about the blankets."

Those must have come later, after their baby died.

"Understandable that she'd do those things. Lots of other volunteer work. She's a fine woman. A man could do worse."

"She doesn't like me much."

"Is that a fact?" Doc scratched at his ear. "She or her mother sit with Helen during chemo whenever I can't be there. Guess you didn't know that either."

Jake shook his head. "I didn't, but I'm not surprised. She's got a big heart." For everyone but him. Except lately, she was even nice to him.

"Helen gathers a lot of information from their talks and I can tell you, son, Rachel doesn't hate you. I'm sure you've noticed she never remarried. Never had those kiddos the two of you wanted."

"I've wondered about that. She says she never found the right guy."

Doc gave him a long look. "Maybe she did. Once."

Jake heard what Doc didn't express.

Was he the reason Rachel had never found love again? Had their breakup so damaged her heart that she was afraid to give her love away to someone else?

His stomach rolled, sick at the thought of someone as wonderful as Rachel avoiding the things she'd always wanted most.

"She carries a lot of pain, and she might be mixed-up some right now with you coming back home after all these years, but animosity is not Rachel's problem."

He knew that. Deep inside, Jake knew Rachel didn't hate him. He didn't know exactly where they stood, but he wanted to find out.

A couple of times this week, Rachel had dropped in to check on Moose who played his injury to the hilt, loving the extra attention. They'd taken the dog for slow, clumsy walks down the block and back.

One night she'd even brought Easter committee work and they'd stuffed plastic eggs until he had dreamed about them.

He tried to tell himself her visits were for Moose or Daley or the Easter event, but he knew better. Rachel had softened.

Something brewed. But was she interested only in friendship? When Moose was well and Easter passed, would Rachel disappear again?

He hoped not. He could not bear the thought that she was still alone because of his mistakes.

"So," Doc said, going back to his half-emptied box of

wormer, "if folks get a thrill out of seeing the two of you together, maybe they see something you and Rachel don't. Yet."

Putting a box of syringes on a shelf with the label turned outward, Jake asked the question that had been on his mind for days. "Are you in on it too? This matchmaking conspiracy?"

Doc laughed. "Now, Jake, I never said a word about matchmaking. Sure never mentioned a conspiracy. Sounds like a spy movie."

Jake chuckled. "No, but you've spent plenty of time singing the praises of my ex-wife."

The older doctor pointed a rugged finger at him. "That's 'cause I don't want a blind man stocking my medicine cabinet."

While Jake pondered the comment, the front bell tinkled, announcing another patient.

"Somebody's here. Better go see." Doc pushed the wormer box toward Jake.

"Mandy will check them in."

"I'm leaving at eleven, so I'll take this one. Helen's not feeling well and I promised to take her some ice cream. Funny how she can't keep a thing down but ice cream sounds good to her."

Doc took such loving care of his sick wife. Jake prayed every night that God would spare Helen's life and heal her body.

"Why didn't you say something earlier? Go home. I'll handle any patients that come in."

"Nah, eleven is okay. You finish up here and treat the rest when I'm gone."

After Doc hurried toward the front, Jake finished emptying the box of wormer, thinking about their conversation.

So, there *was* a conspiracy to get him and Rachel together again. A scheme by well-meaning friends and neighbors to give them another chance to make peace.

Wasn't that what he wanted more than anything? A chance to resolve the heartache they'd caused each other? A chance to heal the still-raw wounds?

As he finished shelving the drugs and filling the drawers, Jake knew he wanted those things and more. He wanted Rachel to forgive him and to love him the way he loved her.

At noon, Jake locked up the clinic and texted Rachel that he and Daley would pay Moose a visit and then be on their way to pick her up.

Not one surgery patient or emergency had detained him.

Rachel replied to this text with a double smiley face that left him buoyed and looking forward to the next few hours.

He hadn't expected this camaraderie to happen, but he was glad. Doc was right, and the matchmakers were right, whoever they were.

He and Rachel needed to resolve their differences. The two of them together again as friends. Or more.

Did she feel the same building excitement to see him?

Oh, he hoped so.

After the conversation with Doc, he'd prayed about the situation right there in the medicine room and asked God to help him be the man Rachel deserved. To heal Rachel's heartache and set her free to love again. Even if he was not her choice.

This week had been different between them. No doubt about that. Pizza night had broken the ice, and the promised shopping trip gave him an excuse to talk to her.

Twice, he'd stopped at her place to tell her something funny that had happened in clinic. He could always embellish a good cat story to make her laugh or roll her eyes.

Each day, he'd texted her good morning and then felt

charged up and ready to face wild cows and highly annoyed cats when she responded in kind.

A simple "good morning" wasn't much, but he claimed the greeting as progress. He loved knowing that he could still make her laugh.

Humming under his breath with Daley bouncing behind him in her car seat, he drove to Rachel's house, picked her up and headed into town.

She looked springtime pretty this afternoon, sitting in his passenger seat. Shiny brown hair swept the shoulders of a purplish-pink top that tucked into white ankle jeans and accented her curves. Yeah, she had nice curves. Not the girlish figure of old but attractively mature. He wouldn't be male if he didn't notice.

"Lunch?" he asked. "Or shopping first?"

"Shop. Shop," Daley cried, kicking her legs against the back seat.

"Stop kicking, Daley. You're bruising your old man."

The kicking stopped.

Rachel smiled toward his daughter in the back seat. "Are you excited?"

"Yes. I want a bunny and a dress and a baket."

"Don't forget the chocolate."

Daley's giggle filled the truck cab.

Jake got the sweetest feeling when Rachel focused on his child.

They'd bonded, those two. He wanted to tell Rachel what Daley had said about her but was afraid of scaring her off.

As a dad, he ached for what his baby girl did not have. Though he showed Daley photos and videos, and took her to see her maternal grandfather in Dallas whenever he could, her memory was empty. She had no connection with Mallory. She did with Rachel.

"We women would rather shop than eat anytime," she said. "Unless you're starving."

"I can wait. A vet's life is fitting in food whenever he can, and today belongs to you girls." As if to give the lie to his words, his belly growled like a bear.

Everyone in the truck laughed.

Rachel pointed down the street. "Let's stop at the Rise and Shine and grab a snack first."

"Now you're talking. And for that extreme kindness, I'll buy your dinner later."

When she didn't argue, Jake knew this would be a good day.

It was.

Rachel couldn't remember when she'd enjoyed an outing this much. Since there were limited clothing stores in Rosemary Ridge, the shopping trip was shorter than if they'd driven into Centerville or over to Lakeside. Jake wanted to shop local, a chance to get better reacquainted with the towns and businesses. Rachel was good with that. She loved her little town and didn't want to lose any of their homegrown shops.

After a quick look through the choices at other stores, they'd ended at Beverly's Boutique.

Daley was smitten the moment she saw the ruffled pink dress in the window. The child had hopped up and down until Jake teased her about not needing a bunny because she was one.

Jake settled in what Beverly called the waiting chair and left the shopping to Rachel. He knew *she* enjoyed clothes shopping. She knew *he* only endured it.

With the comfort that could only come from having once been together for more than seven years, Rachel took charge.

Unsure of size in a growing child, Rachel helped Daley try on several dresses until they found the perfect fit.

Standing behind Daley, who stared at her reflection in the mirror, Rachel put her hands on the toddler's shoulders and smiled. "You look like a princess."

"Daddy says I *am* a princess. Do you think I am, too?"

"Yes, the very best kind. Your daddy's princess."

Jake was terrific at positively affirming his little girl. As a woman whose dad was gone for work during most of her growing years, Rachel appreciated Jake and Daley's closeness.

"He's right. Let's go show him how pretty you look."

With a bounce in her step, Daley exited the dressing room and rushed to her daddy's chair. Jake, scrolling through his phone, looked up.

"Ta-da!" she cried, arms flung wide as she spun in circles to flare the full skirt. "Buy it, Daddy. I wike it."

She folded her tiny hands beneath her chin in a prayer-like plea that was so cute, Rachel would have bought the dress if Jake hadn't.

"Done." Grinning, Jake pocketed the cell phone and stood to his feet.

Daley took another spin and stumbled into Rachel.

Laughing, she righted the child. "We'd better change so we can pay for this."

"And not ruin that dress before Easter," Jake said.

"There is that." Rachel quirked an amused eyebrow.

"Ready to go?"

"Oh, we're not done. She needs shoes to go with the dress."

He widened his eyes in a comical look. "Her sparkly sneakers won't do?"

Feeling good, having fun, enjoying the give-and-take banter with Jake, Rachel escorted the child back into the dressing room to change. This is what life would have been like if she'd had a daughter. Shopping together. Choosing the right dress for special occasions.

Instead of the grief she expected, Rachel felt blessed to be here with Daley. Any child was a gift, even a child who was not her own. That she was Jake's daughter made Daley special.

There. She'd admitted the truth she'd avoided for weeks. Regardless of their ending, Jake held a special place in her heart.

Though Rachel feared where that admission might take her, she could not deny her feelings any longer.

When they exited the dressing room, Daley once again in casual clothes and sneakers, Beverly waited, the lavender-print dress extended toward Rachel. "Try this. It's you."

Rachel fingered the silky spring material. "It is beautiful."

"Go on. We have time." This from Jake, his gaze settling on her with steady encouragement.

"Why not?" With an excited twitter in her veins, she hurried into the dressing stall.

Moments later, she stared at herself in the mirror. The dress fit the way she liked and felt gorgeous on. She couldn't deny that lavender was a favorite color that brought out the purple color in her gray eyes. Jake had always said so.

Jake again. Did she want to look pretty for him?

Stroking her hands down the sides of the smooth-fitting garment, Rachel mentally argued the need for a new outfit. She had plenty of clothes.

But when had she bought anything new for a special day like Easter?

From outside, Jake's voice broke into her inner argument. "Come out when you're dressed. We want to see."

Feeling self-conscious, she slowly stepped out. Did she look as nice in the dress as she thought?

"Wow." His lips formed a silent whistle. "Oh boy. Wow."

"You think?"

"Yes." He spun his finger over his head for her to turn. "Beautiful."

The light in his eyes set off all kinds of wild thoughts and emotions inside Rachel. She recognized that look. Admiration. Affection.

To Beverly hovering nearby with a happy smile, he nodded. "We'll take it."

The *we* shook her. There was no *we*. Was there?

Did she want there to be? Was a relationship even possible when the sorrowful topic of the past hovered like a black buzzard?

Embarrassed, uncertain, but yearning for something more than a new Easter dress, Rachel did a slow turn, executed a playful curtsy and then rushed back into the stall.

Chapter Fifteen

The Drug Store Café bustled with Saturday energy and the scents of grilled burgers and fried chicken. Though Rosemary Ridge boasted other eateries, including a nice restaurant on the edge of town, the café's Main Street location made for an easy stop when downtown. The throwback ambiance was nice too. High tin-plated ceilings, old-time soda counter and clear apothecary jars filled with candy reminded visitors of the building's original business a hundred years prior.

With Daley hopping as she clung to one of his hands and his opposite fingertips riding lightly at Rachel's back, Jake chose a booth toward the rear of the old building to give Daley room to move. His child had behaved perfectly today, but she'd also missed her nap and Jake was taking no chances of a meltdown over a plate of mashed potatoes.

He'd expected to be bored by the shopping trip and tired afterward. He was neither. Energy matching that of the café surged through him.

As they were seated, Rachel and Daley on one side and Jake on the other, Rachel commented, "The Mary Janes are perfect shoes for Easter, but I forgot about tights."

He screwed up his face as if he had no idea what she

meant. He did. Those long, thick panty-hose things that kept Daley's legs from freezing off on cold days.

"Tights?"

She batted at him. "Oh you, you know what tights are."

"I gots tights, Miss Wady." Daley held up two fingers. "Free of them."

Jake reached across the table and raised the third finger. "That makes three, Daley. You're three." He tapped each tiny fingertip. "One, two, three."

"Uh-huh. Yeah. I gots free." This time she pushed the third finger up and smiled proudly.

"Any white ones?"

"Uh-huh. And bwack."

"Somewhere," Jake said. "I'll find them before Easter."

"Still haven't finished unpacking?"

"I have. But I don't always recall where I put everything."

"Understandable. Reorienting takes time. When I moved into the townhouse, I put some things in storage and then couldn't remember which were in storage and which were somewhere in the townhouse."

"Did you ever figure it out?"

Her lips lifted at the corners, drawing his attention to her mouth. He loved her smile. And those lips. "Not yet."

"The Bundt pan's still lost?" he asked, mainly to make her smile again.

She did, and his chest swelled like a hot air balloon.

They sat there grinning at each other, and the moment stretched, feeling incredibly good.

The waitress arrived and took their orders. Rachel, he noticed, still preferred chicken and he still loved a good steak. Catfish Myrick, he'd heard, could grill a steak to make a grown man cry. Jake was about to find out.

Daley wanted chicken like "Miss Wady's," so he'd ordered her a child-sized version.

The bond between those two grew with every meeting. He prayed this was a good thing. He did not want to see his baby hurt, though he could not imagine Rachel ever intentionally causing disappointment to a child. She loved kids. Always had.

"Today was a good day." Rachel leaned back against the booth and worked a kink out of her neck.

"You're tired."

"Not really. Are you?"

Daley tilted against the wall and yawned.

"Someone at this table is, but not me."

His daughter popped up straight. "I not tireded, Daddy. I hungy."

Jake exchanged amused looks with Rachel. "She's never tireded. Until she falls asleep right where she is."

"Trying on clothes and shoes is hard work for a three-year-old, but I'm convinced she enjoyed every moment."

"She did. Didn't you, sprout?"

Brown ponytails bobbed up and down. One had loosened and slid slightly sideways. "Let's go again a-morrow."

"Tomorrow's church." Jake patted the top of her hand. "Your friends would miss you if you weren't in Sunday school."

Daley turned her charm on Rachel. "Are you going with us, Miss Wady?"

Right then, the drinks arrived and were sorted around.

But Jake wanted an answer to Daley's question.

When the server left, he sipped his sweet tea and then set the glass on the coaster. "You can ride with us. Lunch after."

Rachel hesitated. Jake held his breath.

"Do you think that's wise?"

"The town is talking anyway, if that's your concern." Though he knew the other thing, the subject he was afraid to bring up, was part of the reason. "What can I say? I like sitting next to you in church."

A look of pleasure passed over her features. In a quiet voice, she admitted, "The best of times."

Jake wondered if they'd crossed another threshold today, so he pushed the advantage. "Nine forty-five? Sunday school at ten?"

He knew she taught a class but they'd be together in the main church service. Meeting her in the foyer, walking her to their seats, worshiping together. Yeah. He wanted that.

Lips pressed together, Rachel seemed to consider before finally saying, "I invited Mom over for pot roast after church. You and Daley could join us. If you want to. No pressure if the idea seems awkward."

"I want to." Would he feel awkward eating Sunday dinner with her mother present? Maybe. Did he care? No.

Not one bit.

Later that evening, with Daley passed out in her car seat from happy exhaustion, Rachel hurried across the grass toward her townhouse with Jake at her side.

Drizzle had started while they were in the café and now fell in a light rain that dampened the grass. The irritating Oklahoma wind had died down for the night, and the temperature had cooled.

She was still pondering the wisdom of inviting Jake to Sunday dinner. What would Mom say? Would she tease? Or worry? Or was she the one pushing for a reunion between them?

"Been a long time since I walked a girl to her door after a date," Jake said when they reached her porch and stood beneath the overhang.

A giddy tingle raced over Rachel's skin. This wasn't exactly a date, but she'd enjoyed every minute. With Daley. With Jake.

He was still Jake, and even if they had never been married, she would have called him friend today.

Now, with the soft patter of rain on the porch roof and the pleasant outing behind them, nostalgia threatened to overtake her.

Whether she'd intended to or not, she liked this man very much.

Considering what she knew that he didn't, was she setting herself—and him—up for more heartache?

"Walking me to the door wasn't necessary, Jake. Especially in this rain."

"Aw, what's a little spring rain? I kind of like it."

"You always did."

"So did you. Remember how we used to look forward to rainy days without lightning so we could take a walk?"

That nostalgia thing again pecked away. Gentle rain, romantic walks, joy in simply being together.

"I haven't done that in a long time." Not since the last walk with Jake.

In the dim light from the street and his headlights, Jake pulled a wry face. "Me neither, unless you count the vet calls in torrential downpours when a cow decides to calf in a creek."

"The glamorous life of a veterinarian?"

"Right. I'd rather walk with you in the misty rain. Or even in a hurricane."

Rachel tried not to react to how intimate that sounded. "We don't have hurricanes."

"But we have this." He motioned toward the soft fall of precipitation beyond the small porch overhang. "If Daley wasn't asleep in the truck, I'd take you for a stroll right now."

"And we'd laugh at our wet faces."

"And chase each other around the park's merry-go-round." His smile grew as nostalgic as Rachel felt. "I always caught you."

Steeped in the happy past, Rachel put her hand on his chest and gave a little push. "Because I let you."

His hand captured hers and pressed her fingers against his shirt. She could feel his heart beating, steady, strong, dependable. Like him.

"Jake," she warned.

"Rachel," he mocked but slowly drew her closer, his eyes holding hers captive.

She should move away, unlock her door and rush inside. She didn't.

"Jake, I don't know…" But she didn't pull away.

"I do. I want to hold you, kiss you."

Rachel swallowed. She wanted that too.

Had she so easily lost her good sense?

When she moved into his embrace, he sighed as if in relief and whispered, "You always smell so sweet."

Jake smelled of spring rain and cotton, a heady combination that stirred a dozen good memories.

They stood that way for long moments, content to be held, though a thousand thoughts raced through Rachel's head. Confused but content.

The gentle shower provided soft music, the walls of the townhouse porch a refuge for two aching hearts that remembered each other but also remembered the sorrow.

When a car turned the corner and accelerated down the adjacent street, Jake moved them deeper into the corner of the porch.

Softly, he murmured, "Talk of the town."

The words amused Rachel, and she lifted her face to his. "There's an old song about that."

"Yeah?" he murmured, moving closer and closer until she knew he would kiss her, and she wanted him to.

"Bonnie Raitt."

His mouth curved. "Let's give them something to talk about? Sounds good to me."

Then his lips met hers, warm and firm and familiar. Even after such a long separation, she had not forgotten the special beauty they'd once shared. Something awakened inside her heart that she'd ponder later. Right now, Rachel let herself enjoy the moment.

When the kiss ended, Jake smiled tenderly down at her with affection and whispered, "Good night, Rachel. Lock your doors."

Then the only man she'd ever loved walked out into the rain and left her reeling and wondering how to stop a runaway train like the one she'd boarded tonight.

All day Sunday, Rachel wrestled with her thoughts. Letting Jake back into her life meant facing the demons that haunted her. But seeing him again also meant feeling the giddy joy that she'd awakened to that morning. It meant enjoying the pleasure of his, and Daley's, company at church and then at dinner on Sunday afternoon.

Mom had been as gracious to Jake as if he'd never been gone. They'd laughed, talked and played games with Daley. At Rachel's request, Jake had even brought Moose over. He was a hero and received attention accordingly.

Except for her misgivings, the day had been nearly perfect.

As the next week progressed, she found herself agreeing to three more dinners, one at her house, two at his, although she'd cooked one of the latter in her Instant Pot, a machine Jake decided he needed to own. So they went together and bought one and she taught him how to use the appliance. The next day, he impressed her with a dinner of pepper steak and rice. He was so proud of his "culinary expertise," as he put it, she'd had to laugh.

By Friday evening, Rachel eagerly loaded her car with a variety of materials required to set up the park for Saturday's Easter events. Colorful twine for marking off egg-hunting space for each age group. Several trash bags filled with stuffed plastic eggs. Since she and her committee, including Jake, were in charge of the activity, she didn't concern herself with the other events like the parade. Sarah Ambruster had those in her iron hand.

Claire, Wink Myrick and her other committee members arrived, also carting bags full of plastic Easter eggs for hiding in the open areas of the tree-and-flower-lined city park. The local garden club kept the area blooming and beautiful, a perfect place for outdoor events.

Jake arrived soon after, still in his blue work scrubs.

"You could have gone home first to change. We'd handle this," she told him.

Stepping close, Jake squeezed her shoulder and smiled down at her. "Couldn't wait to see you."

Rachel glanced about to see if anyone had noticed. Though Claire should have been stringing bright blue twine for the preschool age, the watchful best friend grinned at Rachel.

"We gave them something to talk about, all right," she muttered, uncertain about the stares and smiles.

"I don't care. Doc says seeing us friendly again makes them happy. Don't you want to be part of making people happy?"

When he put it that way… "Where's Daley?" She'd almost said "our girl," but stopped in time to avoid making a fool of herself.

"My parents' house in Lakeside. Daley likes to hang out with Gram and Gramps, ride in the boat, and feed the ducks. They spoil her."

"She's easy to spoil."

"That's what Mom and Dad say, and they're coming tomorrow for the big events anyway, so she's sleeping over." He rubbed his hands together. "I am a free man tonight, so where do I start, boss lady?"

She handed him a ball of orange twine. "Orange for the teens. Find your group and help them rope off their area. When they're finished, send them home so we can hide their eggs. No cheating!"

"Aye, aye, captain." He offered a wink and a flirty salute that set her heart aflutter.

How silly of her to get all worked up over a wink and a smile.

In spite of her internal caution, their kiss on the rainy porch danced on the edges of her thoughts. That one moment had opened the door, and since then, he'd kissed her good-night every time they had dinner.

"Dates," he claimed, "should end on the happiest possible note."

Theirs certainly had, although she went home with a mix of pleasure and turmoil.

Watching Jake gather a group of high school kids, Rachel touched her lips. He was good with the teens. They liked him. One of the boys poked a playful fist at Jake's shoulder. He feinted to one side, jabbed back, missing on purpose and the teens guffawed.

"Earth to Rachel." Claire bumped her from the side. "He's cute. He's nice. He's successful. Go for it."

"Hush. You know better."

"Apparently, he doesn't."

"We're friends, neighbors."

Claire blew a raspberry. "One of these days you'll stop being scared and appreciate what's right in front of you."

"I do appreciate him. I'm also being very careful. Now, go stuff an egg…or something."

With an eye roll, her best friend returned to her group.

Rachel surveyed the park where dozens of volunteers labeled areas and scattered eggs in every nook and cranny, under trees, in patches of grass, around playground equipment and anywhere else they could find to hide one.

Around the western perimeter, other volunteers erected tables and makeshift booths for refreshments and games. One of the Myrick brothers toted a stack of gunny sacks to the supply booth in preparation for the sack races, always good for plenty of laughs and fun.

Food trucks were scheduled to arrive in the morning, although one smart vendor was already in place and filling the air with delicious, tempting smells.

Mrs. Ambruster seemed to be everywhere, directing, bossing, making certain the event came off without a hitch. She was a drill sergeant, but the end result was worth doing whatever she commanded. At the moment, Sarah assisted a pregnant Zoey Chavez in erecting signs and banners. Rachel didn't know Zoey very well, but she lived with a well-liked foster mom whose health was failing. Other volunteers pushed the pointed sticks of decorative plastic bunnies, ducks and chicks into the soft ground along the sidewalks and near the fence fronting the highway.

The atmosphere was exuberant. Tomorrow would be even more exciting and she couldn't wait, especially to watch Daley carry her new pink-and-green Easter basket as she hunted eggs with the other toddlers. Photos were a must.

As if of their own accord, her eyes found Jake. He and a couple of teenagers with a roll of wire had broken away from the rest of the group to erect the petting zoo pen. Next to that, the animal shelter organized a table announcing free pet adoptions. Tomorrow morning's parade would end here at the park, ushering in a crowd for the afternoon events.

Right now, the park looked and sounded chaotic, but she knew from experience that the event would come together.

Going to her car, she opened the cargo hatch and reached in for the stacks of Easter baskets she'd collected.

"You planning to fill all those? Kind of greedy, aren't you?"

At the deep, unexpected male voice, Rachel startled and yanked herself out of the vehicle, barely missing a whack on the head. "Where did you come from? I thought you were working on the petting zoo."

"Noticing, were you?" Jake pumped his eyebrows.

"Oh, hush."

Grinning, Jake reached around her into the cargo hold and removed a stack of baskets. "I was noticing you."

Pleasure warmed her belly. "I collected these extras in case some kids forget theirs."

"Or can't afford one. I know you. Taking care of the world."

"I don't want anyone left out."

"Me either. Come on. Show me where these go and then come look at the petting zoo. Give me your opinion."

Side by side they walked to the supply booth manned by their church and dropped off the baskets. More than a few glances slid in their direction.

Rachel tried to ignore them, but when Jake, his hands now free, wrapped his fingers around hers, she didn't know what to do. If she jerked away, she'd hurt his feelings and cause more gossip. If they walked around the park holding hands, the whole town would think they were back together.

In spite of her misgivings, she couldn't embarrass Jake by pulling away.

Besides, his skin against hers, his touch, felt too good to let go.

Chapter Sixteen

When the park was decorated and eggs carefully dispersed all over the place, Police Chief Ambruster stopped by to assure everyone, especially his wife, that one of the patrol cars and a couple of officers would keep a watch on the park and decorations tonight and during tomorrow morning's parade.

Jake was glad to hear that. He'd been concerned about ornery kids or mean-spirited adults destroying the hard work under cover of darkness.

Now, as he walked Rachel to her car, they discussed that very thing and the excitement tomorrow would bring.

"I need to drive out to Fespermans' bunny farm," he told her. "She called while I was checking out the food-truck hot dogs. One of the rabbits she planned to bring tomorrow is behaving 'funny,' to use her word. I want to have a look to be sure he's healthy enough for the zoo."

"Can't you do that tomorrow when she brings the bunnies into town?"

"I'd rather check out the problem now. If he's sick, others could be sick too."

"We can't have that in a petting zoo full of children."

"Want to come with me? I'd enjoy the company."

After a brief hesitation while he held his breath, Rachel finally nodded. "I'm too keyed up to sleep anyway."

The drive to Fespermans' farm took fifteen minutes. Now that he'd refreshed his memory on the country roads as well as the location of farms under Doc's care, he no longer required Rachel's navigation but he sure liked her company.

On this trip, so different from the other one to Fespermans', Rachel didn't hug the passenger door with cold aloofness. She chatted easily about Easter, about Daley's excitement and how much they both looked forward to watching his little girl hunt eggs and enjoy the festivities.

Nice, Jake thought, *to feel this comfortable with Rachel again*.

When they arrived at the farm, Mrs. Fesperman met them in the yard.

"This way." Terse and clearly concerned, the hearty farm woman led the way toward the rabbit barn without further conversation. Her plaid flannel overshirt flapped behind her as she picked up her pace.

Jake and Rachel exchanged glances as they followed. Concern ratcheting, Jake held his bag in one hand. His other rested on Rachel's elbow. Touching her grounded him in ways he couldn't describe but knew had been missing in his life for a long time.

He loved her. Could she ever love him again? He prayed about her daily, about them. Everything in his spirit believed God had called him back to Rosemary Ridge to mend the brokenness between him and Rachel.

Only, he wasn't sure how far that mending was meant to take them.

To forever, he hoped. Prayed. God hadn't been exactly clear about that yet.

He caught the thought and turned it over in his mind.

Since Mallory's death, he'd been convinced of his failings and that he should never even consider marrying again. He'd not been enough husband for either wife.

His heart skipped a beat.

Was he considering a full reunion with Rachel? As in, destination marriage?

"It's Alphie. He's acted funny all day, not moving around like normal. I sequestered him in case he's contagious."

Jake jerked his attention back to the farmer. They'd reached the rabbit enclosure, and with the lights on, he could see the large white rabbit sitting sadly alone in one corner of the hutch. "Any other symptoms? How's his appetite?"

As he listened for the answers, he removed his stethoscope from his bag.

"He's not eating much."

"But still eating?" Near constant nibbling was important in rabbits. A loss of appetite could mean real trouble in a hurry.

"Only his favorites, like romaine and turnip greens. It's not a blocked gut, is it?" A blocked gut was an emergency in the rabbit world.

"Let's give him a listen to be safe." He pressed the stethoscope bell gently into the bunny's soft belly to rule out ileus.

With a relieved sigh, he reassured the farmer. "His belly is not the problem. Let me look him over and see if I can find anything."

Mrs. Fesperman brought a flood lamp closer while Jake searched the animal for any outward sign of illness, including fleas, mites, cuts or bites.

He was aware of Rachel at his side, watching him work while she soothed the lethargic bunny. Occasionally, their fingers brushed and he thought sure an electric current raced up his arm. Fanciful, maybe, but Rachel affected him on all kinds of levels.

When he reached the rabbit's hind legs, he found the problem. "Shine the light on his left hock. See this tiny bald patch? His hock is sore."

"That little place can make him sick?" Rachel stroked the rabbit soothingly.

"Rabbits put a lot of pressure on those hind legs and if something rubs him the wrong way, he'll pick at his fur, and this bare, sore patch results. He doesn't want to move because the pressure of moving hurts."

"How did I miss that?" The robust farmer leaned close, a fist perched on one hip. "I looked him over good before bothering you."

"A bit of missing fur is hard to see sometimes. Don't beat yourself up. Your rabbits are among the healthiest I've ever seen." He removed a spray cleanser from his bag and began to gently irrigate the irritated area. "I'll leave this spray and some antibiotic ointment." He gave her detailed instructions on caring for the rabbit. "Let this fellow stay home tomorrow and rest up, but the others should be fine for our petting zoo."

Taking the medications in hand, Mrs. Fesperman wagged her head. "Doctor, I can't tell you how relieved I am. My rabbits are my babies. I'm sure sorry about calling you out this late."

"Not a problem." In fact, he was glad for the excuse to spend more time with Rachel.

Once the rabbit care was completed, he and Rachel headed back into town.

"Hungry?" He glanced toward his passenger.

"Not really. I had a hot dog from the food truck."

"Me too." He'd already told her that, but he was disappointed. The night was young. He wasn't in the least tired. Quite the contrary, he was energized, probably because of the exceptional company riding in his truck and this wild realization that had sprung into his head tonight.

Rachel twisted in the seat to face him. "I could use something to drink, though."

"Lemonade?" he asked hopefully.

"Lemonade sounds amazing. If you'll stop at the store, I'll run in for lemons."

"No need. I bought a gallon at Chick-fil-A while I was in Lakeside."

Rachel moaned a happy sound. "The best lemonade on the planet."

"Yeah. I wonder what they do to make theirs so good."

"No clue, but if you have Chick-fil-A lemonade, lead on."

He was hoping she'd say that. He'd purposely stopped for the drink with her in mind.

Once at his house, he released Moose from his crate and took him out for a brief visit while Rachel poured their lemonade.

With the retriever lying at their feet, they settled on the couch with the frosty, sweet-tart beverage. Jake clicked on the television but turned the volume low. Background noise served as an icebreaker, though they no longer seemed to need one.

Over the rumble of some detective show he never watched, they chatted about the evening events, the park setup and the sick rabbit. All the while, Jake struggled with the one subject he didn't want to discuss but knew they must if they were ever to progress further.

When a natural lull finally arrived, Jake swigged his lemonade and let the tangy liquid clear his throat.

Next to him, Rachel curled one leg beneath her, her fingers touching his on the back of the cushions, as relaxed as he'd seen her.

He leaned in and pressed his lips to hers. He felt her surprise, though she shouldn't have been.

"What was that for?" Her tone was whispery.

He remained close, searching her face, her eyes for any sign of rejection.

He didn't find any.

"I'm tasting your lemonade."

Those beautiful lips curved. "Does mine taste different from yours?"

"Let me check again." He kissed her a second time. She kissed him back. Warm, soft, tart and sweet, a perfect description of their relationship since his return. He was ready to eliminate the tart for good.

There was only one way to do that.

With his knee touching hers and their fingers now intertwined, he sucked in a steadying breath.

"We need to talk."

Caution flared in her eyes. "About what?"

He took her fingers from the cushion and drew her hand against his heart. "I think you know. About us. About what happened to us before."

Rachel started to pull away. "I don't see any reason to discuss the past. Can't we keep things the way they are?"

Who was she kidding? She'd constantly struggled with their past since his return. But only inwardly. Discussions scared her.

He gripped her hand, his expression tender and desperate at the same time. "Please. Something good is going on between us, but until we clear the air about what drove us apart, we can't move forward."

She stiffened. "Clear the air? *Clear the air?* Jake, you left me. Our baby died and you walked out."

"That's not exactly the way things happened." He kept his tone easy and kind, and she heard the longing.

Rachel closed her eyes. The terrible pain in her chest left her breathless. Her pulse rattled against her collarbone, choking her, threatening panic.

She wasn't being fair. She knew she wasn't, but the angry dragon she'd hidden for years stirred to life and threatened to attack anyone in striking distance. Jake in particular.

To calm the violent urge to lash out, Rachel drew in several calming breaths.

When she had herself under control, she lowered her voice. "I know the fault wasn't all yours. We both made mistakes, but I see no reason to look back and rehash old trouble."

"Rachel, hear me, understand the intent of my heart. I care for you, and I want more than anything in this world to heal the pain I caused you. Don't you get it? We have to look back and find closure if we're ever to move forward."

Rachel softened, her heart pounding erratically in her ears. "Is that what's happening here? Are we moving forward?"

"You tell me. Are we?" He released her hand to gesture around the room. "I want us to. Daley wants us to."

"Daley." More tenderness threatened to choke her. Talking about this hurt, but Daley was a balm. "Jake, she is beyond precious."

"I know. Believe me, I know what a gift she is. I also know she loves you."

Rachel longed to ask if *he* loved her, too, but that was ludicrous, dangerous thinking.

When she said nothing else, Jake urged, "We have to talk. Even if nothing else comes from the discussion except to clear the air and walk away good friends."

After the divorce, she'd bottled up her emotions, believing if she didn't talk about them, the pain would go away. She'd been wrong then. Was she wrong now?

"We were such good friends back then, weren't we?" he asked.

And more, she thought. But friends first, best friends.

Admitting the strength of that earlier relationship was easier than she'd expected. "I've missed that."

"Me too. When our son died, I felt broken in half, decimated. I didn't know what to do anymore, how to make things right again. I was lost."

Their son. The one heartache she didn't want to discuss, though the loss haunted her even more since Jake's return. "So was I."

"I know, and I didn't know how to help you. You curled up inside yourself and wouldn't let me in. When I tried to talk to you or comfort you, you pushed me away." His aching voice echoed the ache deep in her soul.

"God seemed a million miles away," she said. "The Bible says He sticks close, no matter what, but I couldn't feel Him." *Or you.* She couldn't feel Jake's love. Or God's.

That was the worst of it. When she'd needed help the most, neither God nor her husband was there to give it. She'd felt abandoned by them both.

"He was with us all the time, Rachel. Maybe like me, He couldn't reach you. You blocked out everyone, even Him."

Had she? She still didn't know, although after a while, the Lord had seemed to ease back into her life, bringing a measure of peace and comfort. Had her eyes been closed to Him during those awful months of loss and divorce, the way she had been closed to Jake?

Brow furrowed, Jake's expression implored, almost palpable in its intensity. "Have you forgotten the times I tried to talk to you, to be with you, even to pray for you? For us?"

Suddenly, things she'd pushed into the abyss with all the rest of the grief floated to the surface. Jake cradling her sobbing body against him, crying with her but trying to be strong. The times she'd hear him praying at the side of the bed when she simply could not get up and face the world. The times he'd pleaded with her to see the doctor for her depression.

"You spent more time out in the backyard or at work than with me," she said, but then was aware of how petulant the accusation sounded. His distancing still bothered her and served as a defense against her own failings.

Was the divorce all her fault just like the other?

"I had to do something or lose my mind." Jake shifted positions to better face her. "That is not an exaggeration, Rachel. A guy at work made some remark about how we were young and could have more kids. Another said 'heaven needed another angel,' and I wanted to punch them both in the mouth. They meant well, but I was furious and took off the rest of the day to cut wood for Bob Styles, taking my anger out on dead trees instead of humans. There could never be another Samuel. No one seemed to understand that."

The realization hit Rachel hard. She'd known Jake was upset over losing the baby they'd both wanted, planned for, longed for. Now she understood that he'd been every bit as devastated in his own way as she'd been.

"I didn't realize. You never told me any of that."

"I didn't want to upset you more. We're mature enough now to talk and to realize that the tragedy affected us both terribly. Aren't we?" he asked as if expecting her to disagree.

She couldn't.

Rachel pressed her lips together, feeling, thinking. "I've been afraid of talking about Samuel, about that time, but saying his name out loud doesn't hurt as much as I expected."

"Lancing the wound often relieves the pain."

Her mouth curved. "Spoken like a veterinarian."

Momentary humor flashed in his eyes but faded to sadness every bit as quickly. "Can we at least try to remember Samuel with joy instead of heartache? We had great plans and dreams for our little guy, remember? How we laid out his future and imagined who he would be? We even made lists of character qualities we wanted to instill in him."

"We did." In bittersweet memory, Rachel visualized the blue-and-tan nursery and the hours they'd spent together painting the stripes and decorating the walls with happy farm animals. "His room was the perfect baby boy's nursery."

"You made his room that way," Jake said softly, and she realized he'd taken her hands in his, holding them lightly as if willing to let her go if she so desired. "Remember the excitement leading up to his birth? The celebration with our parents and friends? All the preparations we made were fun, weren't they?"

His words sailed her back to a time where life was about as perfect as possible. They'd been happier than any couple she'd ever known. Had she ever been that happy since?

"When we did the gender reveal party and everyone bit into their blue cupcakes, I thought you would levitate with excitement." She'd forgotten that moment and the pure delight on her husband's face when he'd learned he would have a son. He'd lifted her off the ground and twirled them around and around, both laughing in exuberant joy.

"I couldn't wait to be a dad, and I knew you'd be the best mother any child could ever have."

The sweet comment settled in the center of Rachel's heart, a soothing ointment against the angry dragon. A dragon that seemed to have receded into the abyss some-time during the prior ten minutes.

Her smile trembled, aching this time for him instead of herself. "You bought him a baseball glove and bat the week after and hung a shelf to store them on."

She'd forgotten about that too. How many other positive things about Jake had she pushed aside in holding on to sorrow and resentment?

They'd waited years trying to get pregnant, praying for a child. They'd *both* been ecstatic. Not just her. And when Samuel's tiny heart stopped, they'd *both* been shattered.

"I still have them."

Rachel blinked at Jake, uncertain if she'd heard correctly. "What? You do? The bat and glove?"

Jake's dark eyes held hers with such tenderness, tears sprang to her own. Not tears of heartache, but tears of bittersweet recollections, tender and precious.

"Letting go of everything seemed like letting go of him all over again. So I kept them."

The tears fell freely now, running down her cheeks. "I have a confession too."

Jake wiped her tears with his thumbs, but they continued to fall.

"Remember," she whispered, "how we'd started that college fund so our Samuel would never have to lose his dreams for lack of finances the way you had?"

When he nodded, Rachel pressed her lips together to hold back a sob before admitting, "That money remains in the bank."

Moisture glistening in his own eyes, Jake asked, "Seriously? You kept Samuel's savings account?"

"I couldn't bear to part with it. Someday, I thought I might donate the money to something special, but I never did. That savings account was the last of a beautiful dream. So, I understand about the bat and glove."

Both of them had suffered, though she'd been unable to see Jake's agony through the blinders of her own grief.

"I blamed you for being cold and heartless, but you grieved as much as I did. Just in a different way."

"My heart was ripped out. I lost him. I was losing you."

"I felt the same." She tilted her face toward the ceiling, saddened all over again, but this time because of her treatment of a good man. "Why couldn't we talk about this then? Why couldn't we help each other? Why is there this awful shroud of silence around lost pregnancy?"

"I don't know, Rachel, but we're talking now, and I don't want our history to be a wall between us anymore. Will you at least pray about it? About us?"

Suddenly, a truth she'd long ignored hit the center of her chest like a fist. For years, she'd nurtured a lie and pushed aside reality. Since Jake's return, she'd fought even harder against it.

But the truth had been there all along, waiting for her to open her eyes and let him in.

She loved Dr. Jacob Samuel Colter, had always loved him. Jake was the reason she'd never found Mr. Right and remarried.

"What do you say, pretty lady?" Jake pressed his forehead against hers. "Can we try again?"

The rest of what he didn't know, the secret no one knew but her, tried to intervene in the tender moment. Rachel pushed back.

Jake had Daley. He had a child to love.

Regardless of the long-range outlook, being with Jake in the here and now filled an empty place in her. The place no other man had been able to fill.

Stroking the curve of his whiskered jaw with her fingertips, she leaned closer. "I thought we already were."

With a quiet chuckle, Jake's lips met hers. And any misgivings she might have had flew out of her head.

This was her Jake. Nothing else mattered. She'd deal with the rest if and when she had to.

Chapter Seventeen

Saturday, the day before Easter and the day of the city-wide events, dawned sunny and cool, a blessing after last year's damp, windy holiday weekend.

Rachel watched the lively parade with Jake and Daley, admiring the floats and the hats. Daley wore a headband of bunny ears, proclaiming her hat the best of all. Her grandparents had skipped the parade but promised to meet Jake afterward at the petting zoo to look after Daley while Jake worked.

Rachel wondered if he'd said something to his folks about her and if they were avoiding her. She wanted to ask but didn't.

After the parade ended, she and Jake separated, heading to their respective duties.

Rosemary Ridge Park, the only one in town, was alive with excited children running amok. Smiling adults tried to corral them, and the scents of every kind of fast food known to food truck vendors fragranced the air. The atmosphere was like a state fair only better because, as her mother reminded her, Easter was about Jesus.

Jesus. Jake had asked her to pray. Last night, after leaving his home, she'd stayed awake a long time talking to God.

The Bible warned to guard the heart, and so she prayed that God would help her do exactly that. Though she loved Jake, a part of her was scared senseless.

Last night's sweet reunion lingered. They'd broken the lethal silence, and she'd found a measure of peace in discussing their son together. Still, she worried that the other shoe would drop and her heart would shatter all over again.

Determined to be happy, Rachel took a deep breath and inhaled the fragrance of cinnamon rolls. The scent from the nearby food truck permeated her position at the supply booth. Her belly growled, a reminder that she'd been too busy working the event to grab a bite of breakfast.

A harried mother grimaced cheerfully as her children, one clinging to each hand, dragged her toward the bounce house.

"Hi Rachel. Bye Rachel." Jamie, the mom, laughed as they scuttled past.

Envy pinched Rachel. How fun to watch your children embrace the traditions of Easter. A pleasure she would never know. A condition she'd accepted. Until Jake returned sweeter, kinder, mature, more wonderful than ever.

She dared not dream the impossible. Jake and Daley were enough, if she were brave enough to accept them. And if they wanted her.

"Their egg hunt is at ten," Rachel called, but the woman was already surrounded by the bouncers waiting to enter the giant rubber play area. Event times were posted in several areas so hopefully no child missed out.

Lively music pumped into the airwaves from somewhere.

At one end of the roped-off areas, volunteers from the high school art department painted faces. Children with their cheeks displaying bunnies and chicks, crosses, crowns and flowers roamed the park.

Another booth featured a balloon artist, deftly twisting long, skinny balloons into monkeys, poodles and such.

Less than a hundred feet away Jake, wearing a balloon twisted into a circle that someone had perched on his head, socialized with a half dozen teenagers as he made his way to the petting zoo. Like the pied piper, he'd convinced the teens to help supervise the children entering the zoo enclosure.

He was great with kids of all ages.

She thought of the baseball bat and glove he'd kept, and her heart squeezed. Though no child was replaceable, she was glad that he'd been given another, even if that child was not hers.

Maybe she was healing after all.

As thoughts of Daley came, she reorganized the baskets she'd been handing out to the first group of egg hunters, and searched the park for Daley and her grandparents. She had not seen Jake's parents since the divorce. The realization gave her jitters.

Would they resent her presence? Refuse to let her share in Daley's day?

They were good people, but she'd divorced their son, badly wounding him in the process.

Lord, please tender their hearts, if not for my sake, for Jake's and Daley's.

She spotted the older couple and couldn't decide whether or not to approach them. As she struggled inwardly, a family with four elementary-age children came up to her booth for baskets. Rachel knew the dad had been laid off from his job and on the mother's minimum wage salary, they couldn't afford Easter baskets.

Thank You, Lord, for these donated baskets.

Quickly assessing her wares, Rachel chose four of the

nicest woven baskets and slipped a small stuffed lamb and a bag of jellybeans into each one.

The mother's eyes met hers with gratitude. In the dad's, she saw embarrassment. Compassion filled her. The children, innocent as lambs, squealed with delight, chattering with excitement as they walked away.

"Softy," someone whispered close to her ear. "I love that about you."

Rachel turned from watching the needy family to find the balloon-hatted Jake next to her.

"They aren't the only ones in need this year. You wouldn't believe how many of these I've given out already. Times are getting harder for a lot of families." She recalled the dad's shame. "I want to help, but I don't want to take away anyone's self-respect or incentive to work either."

"It's a tough balance. But today is about the kids, so forget the rest."

"My thinking exactly."

"I wondered why you bought all that candy and those stuffed animals." He hugged her from the side. His balloon hat rubbed the top of her head. "I love your big, generous heart."

She leaned against him, resting, content for a moment. "Do you?"

Pretending to whisper something, he nuzzled her ear instead.

Laughing, Rachel batted his chest and pulled away. "Jake Colter, not in public. Especially with that balloon on your head."

"Admit it. You want one too. I tried to enter the Easter bonnet contest, but they wouldn't let me. Meanies." He laughed, totally unrepentant, and checked his phone. The hat in question wobbled like a bobblehead. "Time to find the princess. Her event is in ten minutes."

"I saw them over by the face painting."

He groaned, his head dropping back. "She'll want to wear that paint to church."

"I doubt she'll be the only one, but I think we can convince her that her princess dress deserves a clean face."

"I hope so. Can you break free from here and come with me?"

"Already have my relief worker heading my way." She waved at Claire weaving through the gaggle of people. "I don't want to miss Daley's fun. Who's manning the zoo?"

"Doc's here for a while with Helen."

"Oh, good. Helen doesn't get out much."

Claire arrived, wearing a silly I-told-you-so grin and a T-shirt proclaiming Christ is King, slid behind the table. "Go away. I've got this."

She shooed them with her fingers and a pump of sassy eyebrows.

Best friends could get away with being right.

"She likes that we're friendly again," Rachel told Jake as they moved across the grass.

"I'm pretty happy myself." He held her elbow, using his superior size to navigate a crowd waiting for the funnel cake truck to open for business.

"How do you think your folks will react to us being together?"

He dipped his chin toward the couple and Daley coming into sight around the Easter bunny bean-bag toss. "We're about to find out."

Rachel tensed. Jake must have felt her anxiety, because he squeezed her arm lightly. "It'll be okay."

"Daddy, Daddy, I gotted a bunny face!" Daley hopped from her grandparents to him, her silver sneakers sparkling in the sunlight with every hop, the rabbit-ear headband bopping.

Sure enough, a cartoon rabbit's face had been painted across her little nose. Long pink-and-white ears splayed across her forehead like onion sprouts.

Jake murmured under his breath. "That definitely has to come off."

Rachel snickered, but quickly sobered as Nancy and Mark Colter drew near. How should she act? Should she speak first or wait for them to make the first move?

Acid pooled in her stomach. Her pulse quivered.

Rachel was saved from deciding when Daley threw her arms around Rachel's knees and turned her cute face upward.

"I knew you'd come watch me!" Daley cried as if she hadn't seen Rachel in days instead of an hour ago.

"Hey, what about dear old Dad?" Jake pretended hurt. The balloons on his head wobbled.

Daley didn't seem moved by his impassioned speech or his silly hat. She clung to Rachel's legs. "Do you wike my bunny?"

"You are beautiful, bunny and all." The hedge seemed to be the safest reply.

Aware that the child didn't understand the undercurrents of this meeting between former in-laws, Rachel placed her hands against Daley's small back, hugged the child against her knees and forced her focus up to Jake's parents.

"Nancy, Mark. How are you?" She braced for a chilly reception.

Nancy appeared relaxed and, if not overly warm, at least amenable to conversation. An attractive woman in her sixties, Jake's mom looked fabulously casual in denim jeans and white sneakers with a long beige sweater over a navy T-shirt. "Hello, Rachel. Jake told us the two of you had reconnected."

Reconnected. A good term. "Rosemary Ridge is thrilled to have him back in town as the new vet."

Jake reached for her hand. "I'm happy to be back." Rachel flashed him a quick, questioning glance as he continued. "The timing was right to put the past to rest."

Put the past to rest. She liked that view. Neither of them could ever forget, nor should they. Samuel had been a real child. They'd loved him. *Resting* seemed a better option than forgetting.

Mark, looking tanned and every bit the retired lake dweller who spent hours on his boat fishing, wasn't a loquacious guy. He simply nodded and said, "I agree."

"We both do." Nancy's short, iron gray bob fluttered with the slight breeze. She brushed away a stray lock. "Our granddaughter seems taken with you too. She talks nonstop about Miss Wady. If she and Jake are happy, so are we."

A river of relief flooded over Rachel. "Thank you. I can't tell you how much that means to me."

"And me." Jake squeezed her hand again.

Rachel let the tension ease from her shoulders, her pulse finally settling into a steady rhythm. "Your son is still the nicest man I've ever known."

Nancy patted her shoulder. "We know, honey. I'm glad you finally realize that. Now, let's go watch this girl find all the eggs she can. We've been practicing."

Jake was relieved at the way Mom and Dad had greeted Rachel. Not wanting them to be blindsided, he'd had a long talk with them yesterday, and while they warned him to be cautious, they admitted he was a mature man with a good head on his shoulders. He was thankful they'd never realized that he'd failed at not one but two marriages, that he and Mallory had been on the verge of divorce.

Their major concern, like his, was that Daley was be-sotted with Rachel. They didn't want her heart broken.

Neither did he. Nor did he want his own heart crushed, which could worry him if he let it. Rachel still held that power. He hadn't intended to fall in love with her again. But he had, and now he had to figure out what to do about her. So much depended on Rachel. He hoped she felt the same but wouldn't know until he asked.

The five of them reached the area marked off for Daley's age group. Jake knelt on one knee beside his daughter for a few last-minute pointers on how an egg hunt worked. Although for the little ones, the colored eggs were "hidden" in plain sight on the grass. Finding them would be no problem.

Animated with excitement, Daley said, "I know, Daddy. Gram and Gramps showed me. We played hide eggs a whole, whole bunch."

His mother's indulgent nod agreed.

Since adults were allowed to walk along with a toddler, Jake said to Rachel, "Want to hunt eggs with us?"

The question seemed to take her by surprise. She blinked a couple of times as if off balance before holding up her cell phone. "You and your parents go. I'll snap photos."

His mother put a hand on Rachel's arm. She was a touchy-feely mom, always had been. Jake was especially grateful for her kindness today.

"We'll take photos. You go with Daley. She's talked of little else."

"Really?" Again, Rachel seemed surprised.

"No question. Go. My knees are crying from yester-day's egg hunts in the backyard."

Right then, Jake loved his mom more than ever.

A smile that nearly knocked his balloon hat in the dirt spread across Rachel's pretty face. "If you're sure, I'd love to."

During the next ten minutes, delighted chaos reigned as kids and parents rushed for the easy eggs first. At one point, Daley and another little girl reached the same yellow egg at the same time, and his princess let the other child have it without a fuss. Jake's chest nearly burst with pride.

Hurrying on, Daley bent to pick up an egg, accidentally spilling the contents of her basket—exactly three colorful plastic eggs. Before he could react, Rachel was on the ground to help.

Jake's heart squeezed. He, Rachel and Daley together felt like a family. Did Rachel feel the same? Or was he letting his wants outweigh his good sense?

With each found treasure, Daley stopped to exclaim and show the egg to Rachel and him, declaring the color of each one, and then to wave the egg toward her delighted grandparents. Dad waved back and Mom aimed the phone camera at her. Knowing Mom, she'd take a hundred photos to wade through afterward. Not that he minded.

Daley might not collect the most, but his daughter was having a blast at her first public egg hunt.

When the event ended, parents and children trickled back to the starting point to explore the contents of their eggs.

Most kids fell to the ground and began opening the plastic containers, exclaiming over the piece of candy or the tiny toys inside. However, one little boy was crying, showing little interest in his collection.

Daley noticed right away. Sweet face twisted in concern, she asked, "Why's he crying, Daddy? Is he hurteded?"

Jake had overheard the child's complaint. "He wanted a blue egg and didn't find one."

Daley gazed into her basket and seemed to ponder for a long moment. Then she reached in, took out a plastic oval and asked, "Is this bwue?"

"Yes, baby, that's blue."

"Okay." With renewed energy, she hopped up from her place on the grass and trotted to the little boy. Jake followed, ready to intervene if needed.

Daley dropped the blue egg in the boy's basket and skipped back to him, smiling as big as the sun.

Rachel, who'd followed, too, touched his shoulder. "What a wonderful daughter you have."

Jake bent to hug Daley. "She's pretty incredible, I admit."

He was going to buy that kid anything she wanted today.

Chapter Eighteen

When the afternoon ended and families slowly trickled away, tired but happy with their treasures and the activities, Rachel stayed behind for cleanup.

Today had been a great day. Tomorrow promised to be even better, with the children's church pageant and a beautiful Easter service to celebrate the resurrection. Resurrection Day, her church called Easter, focusing away from eggs and bunnies to the event that changed the world forever.

"I can't wait to see Daley in her Easter outfit tomorrow," she told Claire as they searched the grounds for any undiscovered eggs, collecting trash as they went.

"So how's that going? You and Jake? You're looking very chummy."

"We're friends again." Way more than friends. *Trying again,* he'd said.

Claire guffawed. "Looked like more than friends to me."

Rachel bit her bottom lip, head lowered as she searched. "Yes. I think we are, and I'm scared, Claire."

"Why?"

She wasn't about to tell anyone the full reason for her fear, not even Claire. Some things were too personal. "We failed before."

"You were so young back then, Rachel. Merely kids. You're different people now."

Were they? Was she? She wanted to be. "That's what Jake says."

"Hey. Is someone talking behind my back?"

Rachel and Claire raised their heads at the sound of Jake's voice.

"She's telling me what a slacker you are," Claire said, with a laugh. "And how much she loves your balloon hat."

Grinning like a kid, he tapped the twisted balloon still circling his head in a lopsided band of green. "I knew it. She'll try to take it from me. Just you wait and see."

Rachel rolled her eyes but grinned at his cute antics. Yes, she loved this goofy vet.

"He'll probably wear it to church tomorrow." To him, she said, "Did Daley leave already?"

"She's had all the fun a three-year-old can handle. No nap, remember? Mom and Dad took her to my house. They were tired too."

"Nice of them." She commenced searching for abandoned eggs and trash.

Jake, dragging his own garbage sack, searched with them, walking close enough to Rachel to make her pulse happy.

Claire threw Rachel a few sassy glances but kept her thoughts to herself.

For the next hour, they helped a sea of other volunteers clean the park and break down the booths, boxing leftover supplies for next year.

By dusk, they'd finished, and with car doors slamming and motors cranking, the groups headed home.

Rachel loaded her lawn chair into the back of her car and clicked the remote to unlock. The Hyundai chirped.

Jake, who'd walked her to the car, said, "I'm hungry. Want a real meal at the restaurant?"

Her stomach rumbled at the thought of real food. They'd been too busy today to do much more than grab fair food.

"My funnel cake wore off hours ago."

"I'll follow you to your house and pick you up."

"Sounds like a plan." How easily they'd fallen into a comfortable pattern, as if they belonged together.

The thought stung, bittersweet. They did. But they didn't.

If she told him, she'd break his heart all over again.

A few minutes later, she climbed into the high cab of his truck, with Jake standing behind her. Knowing he was there in case she stumbled reminded her of a Bible verse. She didn't remember exactly but something to the effect that two were better than one, because if one fell down, the other could help them up.

She and Jake had failed to help each other up before. Could they really start over without making the same mistakes?

She wanted to believe they could. But what if she disappointed him again? What if she told him everything and he rejected her again? What if her reality was too much for him to overcome?

After the restaurant meal, Jake took her home. As they exited his truck, a misty rain began to fall.

Rachel held out a hand to catch the moisture. "Thank You, Lord, that this stayed away until now."

Jake grabbed her hand, turning his face up to the sky. "Let's walk."

Rachel scoffed. "Walking is all we've done today."

"Not in the rain." His eyebrows lifted in hopeful question.

As tired as she was, a walk in the soft rain with Jake

energized her. With a bump in her heart, she grinned into his handsome face. "Okay."

"Want an umbrella? I have one in the truck?"

"Not unless you do."

Those eyebrows pumped again. "Let's live danger-ously."

The gentle drizzle dampened their skin but not their spirits. Laughing, teasing, flirting even, they alternately strolled and jogged, chasing each other in a playful game of tag. Each time one caught the other, the penalty was a kiss.

They enjoyed a lot of penalties.

When a puddle formed along the curb of one sidewalk, they exchanged glances and both jumped in at the same time.

Soon, fatigue caught up with them and they strolled slowly, arms around each other, heads together. Being with Jake felt right. They ambled along, damp but content to be with each other. *Content*, a much better word than *happy*, although she felt that way too. Delighted, thrilled, satis-fied in ways she'd forgotten existed.

Jake gave her that. No one else had ever come close.

They neared her block and she slowed her steps, not ready to let go of this special time with Jake.

Beneath a streetlight, they paused to watch the rain-drops sparkle beneath the light. Jake tilted Rachel's chin and met her lips in a long, tender kiss that spoke straight to her soul.

With a sigh, he admitted, "You taste so good. I've missed you, missed this more than I can explain."

Rachel's heart bumped. "I feel the same."

Serious eyes studied her face as if memorizing every line. "Do you?"

"Yes. I do. I've missed you." Admitting the truth cost

her nothing and felt almost as good as his kiss. She tiptoed up and pressed her mouth to his.

With drizzle sliding down their cheeks, they held each other close, each warming the other and reluctant to end the evening.

"I love you, Rachel," Jake whispered, smoothing her wet hair away from her face. "I love you even more than before. Grown-up love, I suppose."

The words no longer stuck in Rachel's throat. "I love you too. I always have."

"Today, watching you with Daley did something to me, right here." He banged a fist against his chest. "You were meant to be a mother."

Rachel's heart stuttered. She'd once thought so too. "I love her, Jake. She's wonderful."

He drew in a long breath, then exhaled, his breath warm against her cold cheek. "I've been thinking, dreaming really, about something since the moment I saw you again."

"About what? Kissing in the rain?"

His lips curved. "Well, that too, but something even better. Something more. With you."

Thunder rumbled in her chest, but she ignored the warning, so entranced by Jake's arms around her, his body close, the tender timbre of his voice. And the look in his eyes, oh my. He loved her.

"Something more?" She touched a hand to his soft beard, loving the curve of his strong jaw, the feel of his rain-cooled skin.

"More Daleys in my life. More kids, girls, boys, I don't care. With you. Only with you, the way we always dreamed of. Marry me again, Rachel, and let's have those babies you wanted."

Rachel stiffened. Anxiety gripped her chest. She couldn't

breathe. Struggling out of Jake's arms, she backed away, fighting for air.

He wanted more children. With her.

"No. No. Don't ask me that. I can't. We can't."

"Rachel, what—" He reached for her, stunned. "I thought you loved me. I love you. What is it?"

"No." Hand to her throat, she spun and ran.

Chapter Nineteen

Shocked out of his head, Jake followed along behind the fleeing Rachel. His athletic shoes pounded the pavement. Puddles splashed as he hurried to catch her.

What had just happened?

Why had Rachel suddenly freaked out after declaring that she'd never stopped loving him? She wasn't making sense.

She loved kids, and unless he was a total fool, she loved him and adored his daughter. All she'd ever talked about when they'd dated in high school and after they married was being a wife and mother. Family, that's all she had ever wanted out of life.

Had that changed during his long absence?

Thinking back to her behavior with Daley and every child she'd encountered today, he didn't think so.

And tonight. Oh, man, tonight had been amazing. He'd felt whole for the first time in years, enjoying time with Rachel, knowing she loved him. He'd believed God was giving him a second chance with his first love, a chance to make up for his wrongs and to turn their disaster into something beautiful again, the way they had been before Samuel died.

Something scared her away. Marriage? Kids? Or was it him? He had to know.

By the time he reached her front door, she'd gone inside, and for once, she'd clicked the lock. He banged on the wood. "Rachel. Let me in."

She didn't respond.

"Kind of junior high behavior, don't you think?" he yelled against the door and gave the wood another good pound. "Open up. We're adults now. If I did something wrong, tell me and I'll fix it."

"You didn't." Through the thick door, she sounded breathy, winded, raspy. Had the run done that to her?

"Then, what? Please, Rachel, let me in."

He pressed his ear to the door, listening. He could hear her breathing. Gasping, actually. He started to worry about her. "Are you all right?"

"Fine. Go…a…way." Her voice was not only raspy, she sounded weaker.

"Not until I know you're okay." And until she explained her sudden change of heart. "Open up. Now."

He slammed a fist into the wood three times, each one harder, hoping the neighbor in the adjoining townhouse didn't call the police.

The lock snicked. The door opened wide enough for her to peer out. "See? I'm fine. Short of breath from the run. That's all. Stop pounding."

Her hand still clutched her throat, her chest heaving.

"You look pale. Let me in. We need to talk."

"No. Go home, Jake. We had a nice dream, but that's all it was. We can't get back together."

"Why?"

"I don't want to. I thought we could be friends again, but even that is not possible." She looked as stricken as he felt.

Friends? After she'd said she loved him and kissed him

like a drowning woman who'd found air? After agreeing to try again?

"I don't believe you."

"Believe it. We're done." She closed the door in his face and clicked the lock, leaving him alone on the porch as shattered as before but far more confused.

Back then, he'd understood her rejection. He worked too much. Ignored her needs. Didn't know how to comfort her or even talk to her about the miscarriage.

Since their reconnection, he'd tried to show her how much he'd changed. He spent time with her and Daley instead of rushing off to work. They'd discussed the miscarriage and he'd thought the discussion brought them closer. Every single day he tried to be a man she could admire again.

So what had caused her sudden change of heart?

When her living room light went dark, Jake headed to his truck, head down, the soft rain no longer pleasurable. Nothing was, without Rachel.

He climbed inside and started the engine, turning the heater to High, but remained in front of her home for several long, aching moments.

As he pondered their evening right up until the time she'd bolted, he realized what he had done. Rachel was fine with being friends. She liked him, maybe loved some part of him enough to kiss him in the rain. But when he'd mentioned marriage, she'd fled.

He banged his head on the steering wheel, wanting to punish himself for being such a fool. Why had he even tried again? Two marriage failures and now a rejected proposal should be enough to convince him forever.

No matter how much he loved Rachel, no matter how much Daley needed a mother, no matter how much he longed to make Rachel his wife, Jake Colter was obviously not marriage material.

* * *

Easter morning dawned with the same dark clouds that filled Rachel's entire being. Jake loved her. She loved him. But they could not be together. Explaining would only hurt him more, so she'd keep that particular heartache inside.

Her mother phoned early that morning before church. "Are you still coming for Easter dinner?"

"Sure." She tried to sound more chipper than she felt. Mom's parental radar could detect a mood a mile away.

"Bringing Jake and Daley?"

"No." Rachel scrambled for a reason, not ready yet to talk about the breakup when she and Jake had barely started seeing each other again. "His folks are here."

"Nancy and Mark are welcome too. You know that. There's always plenty of ham and hot rolls. I made your favorite coconut cream pie." She said the last as if to entice her. Normally, the pie would do the trick. Not today. "Afterward, we'll hide eggs for Daley and Sean's boys and watch the fun. I bought some treats for all three."

Rachel thought her chest would burst. Another panic attack threatened. She took a deep breath and exhaled, counting slowly in her head, the way she'd done last night. She'd said goodbye to anxiety attacks years ago, but she'd almost had one last night, a clear sign that she had to stay away from Jake.

She'd looked forward to today and the fun at Mom's house, but she'd go without Jake and Daley.

"That's generous, Mom, but no. They have plans." Or they'd make some.

"You sound funny. Are you okay?"

The mom radar thing had activated.

"Jake and I aren't seeing each other anymore," she blurted.

An intake of breath, and then in a concerned voice,

Mom asked, "Why not? You looked happy as a clam yesterday. Both of you did. I saw him sneak a kiss. I'd hoped the two of you were back together for good."

Rachel winced. "Mom, please. Let it go."

"All right. I can hear that you're upset, so I'll hold my piece. For now. But I'll be sending up some fierce prayers. See you at church."

They hung up, and Rachel dressed and then attended church as she did every Sunday. As with every Easter, the building was packed. Holding this week's lily-and-cross-decorated bulletin, she slid in between her brother and her mother. Her nephews, both ornery cuties, looked adorable in white shirts and gray vests with blue ties to match their dad's.

In spite of herself, Rachel scanned the congregation. Across the aisle and one row up, Jake and Daley sat with his parents and a surprisingly subdued group of teenagers she'd never seen in church before. Jake's paint crew. Had he invited them? Probably. Bringing kids to Jesus was exactly the kind of thing he'd do.

Heart squeezing at Jake's concern for the teens, she turned her focus to Daley. In her pink princess dress, hair done up in bows and black patent shoes swinging, Daley was a picture of childhood perfection. Rachel hoped Jake had remembered to take photos. Even though she would never see them, she wanted Jake and Daley to have the memories.

Daley spotted her too and pushed off her seat. When Jake leaned down to stop her, she pointed toward Rachel. He looked up. Their eyes met. His were full of wounded confusion. Turning aside, he spoke to Daley and lifted her back onto the chair. Daley's bottom lip poked out.

Throughout the song service, the little girl shot frequent glances Rachel's direction. Rachel tried not to notice, but she did. She also noticed that Jake never looked her way again.

The Easter pageant, complete with older children and teens dressed in first century attire, commenced. Rachel noted the various robes and angel costumes she and Jake had put together. She bit down on her lip. Remembrances of the weeks they'd spent getting reacquainted and falling in love again seemed to be everywhere. Even in the lavender dress she wore.

Tears sprang to her eyes. She bit harder on her lip.

She couldn't think about Jake.

Although her chest ached, she focused on the age-old story of Easter. At the end, as the women in the garden shared the stunning news of Christ's resurrection and the disciples rushed to the empty tomb to see for themselves, the choir broke out in a jubilant, victorious chorus of "Up from the Grave He Arose!"

Rachel stood with the rest of the congregation to sing as the actors departed the stage and the pastor came forward to begin his message.

At first, she heard little he said, although she saw the scriptures from Mark 16 on the overhead screen. Her mind kept replaying last night's scene with Jake.

Halfway through the sermon, Pastor Everly caught her attention.

"The fact that Jesus's crucifixion and resurrection happened in spring was always part of God's plan, one of His many but most important and meaningful symbolic acts. Spring is a time of renewal when the earth awakens, plants are 'reborn,' if you will, and new life appears on farms and ranches. The same was true in Jesus's time. The Bible says Jesus was the firstborn from the dead. A rebirth, a new beginning, not only for Himself but for us, that we could be reunited to the Father through Him. That we could be made whole. As the Apostle Paul mentions in Hebrews, Jesus gives us a choice to be free from the sin that entangles us. A chance to start anew just as the resurrection was the ultimate new beginning for Christ, His disciples, and for the whole broken world, right down to us."

Something stirred in Rachel's spirit at the pastor's words. How she longed to start all over again where the reality of the past didn't hold her captive. She realized then that she'd allowed circumstances she couldn't change to control her life and steal her joy. But how did she make the change? If she let go of the past, would she be letting go of her son? If she let Jake into her life again, would she be hurting him all over again?

Or are you hiding the truth out of fear of rejection?

As if reading her thoughts, Pastor Everly continued, "Perhaps today you need a resurrection in your spirit, a fresh start. Maybe there's something you need to release to Him and let Him carry for you. Let Jesus lead you in the right direction. He will never steer you wrong."

The pastor paced from the podium to the play's empty-grave prop. Above him, the overhead screen portrayed three empty crosses on the hillside.

"Give your pain to God. Tell Him everything. He wants to heal all your heartache and brokenness, repair your relationships, mend your spirit, offer forgiveness. Whatever you need today, Jesus wants to set you on the road to the best Easter and the best future you've ever had. A future of peace and joy and hope. All you need to do is ask Him."

The pastor motioned into the empty tomb and then stretched his arms wide. "The tomb is empty, friends. The Savior is here. Jesus, our resurrected King, waits with open arms right now. Let Him carry your burdens. That's what He died and rose again to do. Won't you pray to Him today?"

A holy hush fell over the sanctuary as they bowed in prayer.

Something powerful welled inside Rachel so that she couldn't hold back the tears. She went to church. She even taught Sunday school classes. But had she ever asked God what He wanted her to do? She'd prayed to understand why she'd lost so much, but she'd never asked for direction or for Him to heal her dysfunctional body. She'd never thought she deserved to ask after she'd mangled her marriage and driven away a husband.

Instead of leaning on Christ, she'd raged at Him, and in the process, she'd shut Him out just as she'd shut out Jake.

Tears of regret flowed. She pulled a tissue from the box beneath the pew.

For a woman who seldom missed church, she may have filled a pew, but she'd ignored the goodness and mercy and power of Jesus to meet her every need.

"I'm sorry, Lord," she whispered under her breath, feeling humble and tender toward Jesus in a way she hadn't felt in years. "Please heal me and show me how to move forward. Guide me, lead me. I've made a mess of things."

Head bowed, hands clasped to her chest, she prayed silently for healing, forgiveness, for Jake, for the hurt she'd caused him.

Gentle music began to play as the congregation continued to pray.

A hand touched Rachel's shoulder. She knew that touch. Her mother was praying for her too. Did Mom suspect the reasons for her contrition? She didn't care. In fact, she was grateful for a mother who read her like a book and cared enough to pray.

As she released everything to God, Rachel felt His Holy Presence, as if a light turned on inside, bright and clear and clean.

What will you do about Jake?

The thought eased through Rachel's mind and she knew God was trying to tell her something. She'd been unfair to Jake. At the very least, he deserved an explanation. Maybe they really could start again. She had to tell him everything. All of it.

Even if he rejected her.

Jake exited the church service, his soul satisfied even if his heart wasn't. He'd prayed about Rachel and come up empty. No matter what happened between them, he'd always love her and want the best for her. Even though he wasn't it.

"Meet you at the restaurant," his mother said. "We've got Daley."

Their Easter meal would be in a restaurant, not the cozy home-cooked gathering he'd wanted with Rachel and her family. Afterward, they'd head home and spend the afternoon hunting eggs with Daley and Moose, although from the gathering clouds, they'd play in the house.

As he waved his parents away, suddenly feeling terribly alone, someone touched his shoulder.

"Jake."

He turned to find Rachel standing next to him, beautiful in the lavender dress they'd bought together. His heart clutched.

"Rachel. Happy Easter. He is risen."

"Risen, indeed." She didn't smile, rather settled her gaze on him with all seriousness. "Can we talk for a minute, please?"

"I'll walk you to your car." He didn't take her hand or put an arm around her the way he would have done yesterday. She didn't want him. The too-short dream of having her in his life again had imploded around him. He wasn't enough for any woman.

Car doors slammed. Engines cranked. Festively dressed children raced from the church, laughing and talking, parents not far behind.

At her car, Rachel leaned her back against the door. "I have to tell you something."

"Listening."

"You're probably wondering why I behaved so weirdly last night." She picked at an invisible thread on her sleeve.

"Didn't sleep much last night trying to figure out what I did wrong."

Her eyes flashed to his. "You didn't do anything wrong, Jake. The problem is all me. I should have told you everything from the start. Once you hear, you'll understand why we can't be together."

"I can't imagine anything that would change my mind about you, Rachel."

She squeezed her eyes shut as if in pain and pressed her lips together. Jake fought not to pull her close and kiss those lips that fit him so perfectly. She didn't want that. Didn't want him.

"I wasn't lying when I said I love you. I do. I love Daley too. A thousand times, I've wished I was her mother."

It was his turn to close his eyes. With a catch in his throat, he murmured, "She loves you. You could be."

"But you want more children."

The comment shocked him. His brow furrowed. "What's wrong with that? I thought you wanted children too?"

"I do. More than anything. But I'm afraid."

He furrowed his brow. "Of what?"

"Of losing them."

The light came on inside Jake's head. He gently gripped

her shoulders. "I understand that feeling. When Mallory was pregnant with Daley, I couldn't enjoy the anticipation the way you and I had with Samuel, because I feared losing another baby."

"But you didn't. You have Daley."

"I thank God every day for her. But there's no reason you and I can't have a healthy child. The doctors said as much."

"They were wrong." While he tried to comprehend her meaning, she turned her face to the side. Her throat convulsed. She licked her lips. "I've never told anyone, Jake. Never. After you left, I was sick. Something was wrong. Blaming stress, I ignored my body."

"What do you mean you were sick? What was wrong? Are you okay?"

A tear trickled down her cheek. Jake thought he'd break in two.

"I was pregnant. You and I were going to have another baby." Her voice broke. "I miscarried. Again." She raised stricken eyes to his. "I lost our second child too."

Her words were a fist to Jake's gut. He sucked in air, nearly breathless. "Rachel. Oh, my love."

He could no longer resist the need to have her in his arms. She came easily to him and leaned her head on his shoulder.

"You're shaking. I love you. I'm sorry. I should have been there for you. I—"

Rachel lifted her head and put a finger to his lips. "You didn't know. *I* didn't know until it was too late. You were gone. The baby was gone." She shuddered in a long breath. "Now you see why I can't marry you."

He wagged his head back and forth in denial. "No. I don't see that at all."

"I can't give you more children. Don't you understand,

Jake? My body doesn't work right. It won't do what a woman's body is supposed to do." Her voice caught on a sob. "Something in me destroys my own babies."

"Rachel, stop. Stop right there." He pushed her back enough to make her look at him. "I love *you*. I love kids, but I wanted more babies for *you*. I wanted to make *your* dreams come true. Not mine. Even if Daley is the only child I ever have, I'm okay. But I want *you* to be the mother who raises her. We don't have to have more babies unless *you* want that and unless God gives them to us. We can even adopt if you want."

Lips trembling, Rachel sniffed and pressed a tissue to her sodden eyes. "Do you mean that? You wouldn't be disappointed or resentful if we didn't have more children?"

"No. I want you, Rachel. You. You are enough for me and Daley."

Rachel stared into the eyes of her beloved, heart singing a new song. Had God really answered her prayers so quickly and perfectly?

"I want you, too," she whispered, hands folded against Jake's dress shirt, which now was damp with her tears. "If you're sure."

"More than anything, Rachel. I thought you didn't want me. That I was a failure at marriage, condemned to be alone without the woman I love."

"You thought I didn't want you? That you were the failure? No, Jake, no. I'm the problem, not you."

"In church today, I prayed for God to forgive my failures."

A lightness flowed into Rachel's being. "I prayed the same and asked Him to direct me and heal me. Renew me."

"I think He heard and answered, don't you?"

Rachel slid her arms around Jake's neck. "I do."

He leaned in close. Though a few churchgoers still roamed the parking lot and the occasional car drove past, Rachel no longer cared if the whole world knew she loved Jake Colter.

"I like those two words," he said. "I do. Will you say them with me in front of a preacher?"

Her lips curved upward. "I will."

"Then, can I text my parents and tell them not to order at the restaurant, that dinner at your mom's house is still on?"

She reached for her cell inside her purse. "I'll text Mom too. I can't think of a better time and place to make a very important announcement. Can you?"

Jake whipped out his phone, his handsome, beloved face shining, his smile huge. "Celebrating a resurrected marriage on Resurrection Sunday sounds like God's perfect timing. We're about to make a lot of people very happy."

"Especially us."

Though the rain clouds hadn't departed from the sky, they disappeared from Rachel's heart, soul and mind.

Peace. Healing. Hope for the future. A renewed heart and a renewed love. Gifts that only God could give on this celebratory day when He had given the greatest gift of all. Himself.

Epilogue

Three years had passed since that Easter of renewal, and today, she, Jake and their family had come full circle back to Resurrection Day. Since the moment of their remarriage, Rachel had lived her dreams, fulfilled and delighted in loving Jake and Daley.

This year, however, God had added even more joy than she'd ever imagined possible. He seemed to love proving people wrong so that He could bless His children. Rachel was so very glad He had.

"About ready?" Jake's warm baritone spoke at her side. She'd felt him come into the room. Her heart always knew when he was close. He smelled wonderful too, of fresh shower and masculine cologne.

Breathing him in, her heart lifted at his presence. Even after three years of marriage, their love grew stronger.

"He's still sleeping," she said quietly.

Jake's arm went around her waist and they both gazed down at the three-month-old boy in the crib. Their rainbow child, as some termed a healthy baby born after miscarriage, a child they hadn't planned, an unexpected surprise that had both thrilled and terrified her. She was too old. Her body had failed before.

This time, she and Jake had held on to each other and leaned on Jesus every step of what seemed to be the longest pregnancy in history. Even if the worst happened again, they made a conscious decision ahead of time to cling to each other and the Lord, to share their pain and to seek help. They would go through every mountain and valley together as one, the way God intended.

But, to their great relief and joy, God had a different plan for this baby. Their tiny son had arrived healthy and strong.

"Matthew, our gift from God," she murmured, thinking of the meaning of their son's name. "I'll never understand why we didn't get to keep our other babies, but I'm thankful God brought us back together and gave us this healthy boy to go with our beautiful daughter."

The last three years had been the most fulfilled and content of her life. Trust and love had done that. And resting in the truth that Jesus had never abandoned her even when she'd held Him at arm's length.

"If there's one thing I've learned through the wonderful surprise of this little boy and our reunion," Jake said, "it's that God is in control and that He holds everything in the palm of His hand. No matter what happens, good or bad, He's got our best interest in mind."

As hard as it was to believe losing two babies was in her best interest, Rachel had chosen to trust in God's omnipotent goodness.

Didn't this healthy little baby born at her age after two losses prove how much God loved her?

Rachel's smile was tender as she lifted her son from the crib and cradled him. "I find such comfort in picturing our other babies in Jesus's arms, cradled close the way I hold Matthew."

"Except they'll never be sick or hurt." He wrinkled his nose. "Or smelly."

Rachel grinned at his wry expression. "What? You don't appreciate dirty diapers?"

"No, but you smell good and, for once, so does Matthew." Jake leaned in and kissed her forehead, fingers light on his son's tiny chest. "I'd love to linger and kiss you some more, but Daley is waiting downstairs with the photographer."

"Moose too." The dog had objected to the bath she'd given him, but he looked shiny and clean for family pictures. Having long since recovered from his injury, Moose now stood delighted sentry over both Daley and her new baby brother.

With Matthew nuzzling sweetly against her neck, Rachel and her husband—a term that still tickled her insides—joined the others downstairs where the photographer had set up an Easter scene.

"I'm glad we started this tradition for our family." Rachel motioned toward the two previous Easter family photos hanging on the wall. This year's picture would include Matthew, their gift from God, in his baby blue My First Easter outfit.

They settled on the pretty garden bench in front of an Easter backdrop, with Daley between them.

Daley, the doting sister, wanted Matthew on her lap, even if he wrinkled her pretty peaches-and-cream dress. She adored her baby brother, was delighted to no longer be the only child, although she still couldn't understand why he'd arrived unable to play. She wanted to hold him every chance she could, and Rachel let her. Daley would always be the daughter of her heart. She loved the precious little girl every bit as much as she loved Matthew.

Moose stretched himself at their feet, a red splash of fur among the pastel eggs and yellow flowers.

The backdrop above their heads quoted her favorite verse of the Bible, the one that had brought her to this perfect moment. *He is risen.*

For indeed, the risen Christ had brought about a resurrection in her own heart, in her marriage and even in her ability to bear a son.

Though she and Jake would never forget Samuel and their other miscarried baby, with God's help and their love and commitment to each other, they eagerly faced the future with joy and hope.

A son, a daughter, a family.

God had turned their mourning into joy.

Reaching behind Daley, she met Jake's hand and squeezed. Their eyes met above their children and she saw her own joy reflected in her husband.

The camera flashed.

"Perfect," the photographer cried.

Yes, Rachel thought, *absolutely perfect.*

* * * * *

Dear Reader,

You probably know her. Or maybe you are her. The woman who lost a baby through miscarriage or stillbirth, a heart-breaking, grief-inducing, and sometimes relationship-ending tragedy that effects a surprisingly significant number of pregnancies. To add to the heartache, couples who experience pregnancy loss are much more likely to divorce than those who experience successful pregnancies, the percentages increasing with the gestational age of the unborn baby.

As grandmother to two babies who didn't survive pregnancy, I witnessed the devastation my daughter-in-law felt, blaming herself, as Rachel in the book does, for being unable to "do what a woman's body is made to do." Her heartrending words led me to write *A Mommy for Easter* and to explore the grief that too-often destroys marriages, a grief that is frequently suffered in lonely silence. Society, and often the parents themselves, simply don't know how to handle a lost pregnancy.

Rachel and Jake, so named for the barren couple in the Old Testament, not only lost a baby, they lost each other. In *A Mommy for Easter*, I wanted to bring them full circle to face the mistakes they'd made and to find solace *together*, as they should have done in the first place.

Easter seemed the perfect season for a book about healing and restoration. I hope you agree and enjoy this reunion love story.

Happy Resurrection Day,
Linda Goodnight